Charmed in an Arranged Marriage

HISTORICAL REGENCY ROMANCE NOVEL

Dorothy Sheldon

Copyright © 2024 by Dorothy Sheldon
All Rights Reserved.
This book may not be reproduced or transmitted in any form without the written permission of the publisher. In no way is it legal to reproduce, duplicate, or transmit any part of this document in either electronic means or in printed format. Recording of this publication is strictly prohibited and any storage of this document is not allowed unless with written permission from the publisher.

Table of Contents

Prologue..4
Chapter One...10
Chapter Two 17
Chapter Three..23
Chapter Four...32
Chapter Five..40
Chapter Six..47
Chapter Seven...53
Chapter Eight 62
Chapter Nine...69
Chapter Ten 78
Chapter Eleven..84
Chapter Twelve...88
Chapter Thirteen...92
Chapter Fourteen 97
Chapter Fifteen...102
Chapter Sixteen 108
Chapter Seventeen 114
Chapter Eighteen 119
Chapter Nineteen 128
Chapter Twenty 135
Chapter Twenty-One 141
Chapter Twenty-Two 150

Chapter Twenty-Three 155
Chapter Twenty-Four 164
Chapter Twenty-Five 171
Chapter Twenty-Six 175
Chapter Twenty-Seven 182
Chapter Twenty-Eight 186
Chapter Twenty-Nine 189
Epilogue 195
Extended Epilogue 200

Prologue

Somehow, the minutes seemed to stretch on for what felt like hours. A calming breeze drifted through the open bay windows, rustling the tendrils of golden blond hair curled at Isabella's temples. She fussed at it with a huff of annoyance, then resisted the urge to rub the back of her neck restlessly. Everything bothered her. The wind, the silence, and especially the fact that she had been sitting in this drawing room for two hours staring at the boring pages before her.

"Don't sigh, Bella," came a drone before her. "It is unbecoming of a lady."

Bella lifted her eyes to the matronly woman perched in her favorite armchair under the window. Her aunt Gertrude Wentworth looked every bit the adorable, motherly lady she pretended to be, but Bella knew better. She'd been in London for only a week now and had already learned that her aunt was more akin to a strict schoolteacher than anything else.

For a moment, Bella considered how best to answer. "Who cares?" came to the tip of her tongue but her aunt would simply launch into a lengthy lecture that would bore Bella half to death. So instead, she murmured, "Yes, Aunt Gertrude."

"And sit up straight!" her aunt snapped, finally looking up from her own book. "How will you find a husband this Season if you slouch like that?"

"If my husband cares about slouching, then perhaps I do not want him."

"Isabella!"

Bella lowered her eyes to her book, flipping a page as she stifled a sigh. "Forgive me," she muttered then sat up straight. She waited until her aunt's heavy stare lifted before she relaxed again.

"You have a lot to learn, Bella, if you want to become the Diamond of the Season," her aunt continued. "Silly things like refusing to sit up straight and sighing every time you feel discontent will only hinder you."

"I know, Aunt Gertrude," Bella droned, only because she knew that agreeing was the quickest way out of this lecture. But she couldn't hide her restlessness. She didn't want to be here. The only reason she'd stopped fighting in coming to London for the Season was because she wanted the chance to visit the British Museum. She would much rather be there than pretending she cared about Shakespeare's sonnets as her aunt insisted.

"You're a beautiful girl, Bella." Her aunt's tone softened. "But that can only take you so far. There are many lovely ladies in London who will stop at nothing to find their perfect match."

"Is that what you did, Aunt Gertrude? Did you stop at nothing to marry?"

Bella might have been mistaken but she could have sworn she saw a flash of sorrow in her aunt's eyes. She instantly wished she could take back her words. Sometimes it was hard to remember that her aunt had once been in love. The loss of her husband was a painful scar her aunt constantly tried to hide.

"My time is long gone, my dear," Aunt Gertrude said softly. She closed her book, resting it on the side table under the window. "Now it is time to focus on creating a future for yourself."

"My future does not have to rest in a—" A crease formed between her aunt's eyes. Bella bit her tongue. "Tell me about those days," she said instead. "Was it any different from now? I'm certain that something must have changed since then."

"How old do you think I am, child?"

"Four-and-eighty?" Bella asked innocently, a playful glint in her eyes.

Her aunt scoffed. "Your insolence will get you in trouble one day, you know. But to answer your question, not much has changed. So, you will do well to listen to me, child. I know what I am talking about."

Sensing another lecture, Bella switched courses. Between listening to her aunt talk about the past and reading another dreadful line of her book, the choice was easy. Still, she left the heavy book in her lap.

"What of Father?" Bella probed. "What was he like?"

Aunt Gertrude sighed softly and nestled further into her armchair. The large orange cat, Mr. Whiskers, that had been lounging by the hearth got to its feet at the sound, ambling over with slow blinking eyes. He jumped into Aunt Gerturde's lap, spun twice, and then curled up to sleep.

"You do not know your own father, my dear?" her aunt asked wearily, stroking her haughty-looking car.

"Not nearly as much as I would like," Bella admitted. "We have been in London for an entire week and I have only seen him once since our arrival. He hardly has any time for me." She didn't mean for her words to sound as bitter as they did. Hopefully, her aunt hadn't noticed.

Aunt Gertrude only said, "Never you mind what your father is doing. He is an important man in the House of Lords, so you needn't worry about where he is. Go on, continue reading."

The older lady twisted to face the window, still stroking her cat as it purred loudly in her lap. Bella stifled another sigh. That was the end of that, she supposed.

Bella resumed her reading, speaking out loud to appease her aunt despite her distaste for Shakespeare's work. The words blended together, her voice nothing but a low hum accompanying the *tick-tock* of the grandfather clock across the room. After a while, Bella hardly heard herself, her mind drifting back to the last thing her aunt said.

He is an important man in the House of Lords, so you needn't worry about where he is.

Easier said than done. She hadn't been able to stop thinking about her father and his state of mind since...since Christopher passed away. The gentleman she'd come to love had hardened into a cold presence Bella could not come to terms with. Even though it had been four years since her brother's passing, her father was still mourning. He would never admit it. No one would. But Christopher's passing left a mark on everyone's heart and only Bella seemed capable of poking her head above the murky water of sorrow.

And her mother...

The Duchess of Redshire was only a shell of her former self, even with the mask she constantly wore. Bella knew better. She saw through the smiles that lifted her mother's lips and the lilt in her voice when she spoke. She heard the sobs at night, shattered gasps and tremors as if her mother had been suppressing it all day.

A pang of longing hit Bella suddenly. Right now, the duchess was still in the countryside attending to Bella's sister, Matilda, who was expecting her first child. Bella had wanted to stay, had begged her father to let her skip this Season. But he was insistent, and once the Duke of Redshire decided something, everyone else had to fall in line.

A distinct nasal sound interrupted her speech. Bella glanced up to find her aunt's head slanted upon her lap, while a resounding snooze reverberated across the room.. She laughed under her breath. *Quite ladylike*, she thought.

She returned her attention to her book, then paused. This was her chance, she realized. Her aunt was a heavy sleeper. This sudden nap could buy her perhaps an hour or two of freedom.

Slowly, Bella wedged her bookmark between the pages and set the book aside, keeping her eyes on her aunt. Even though she doubted she would wake her, Bella rose as quietly as she could, backing away. She didn't so much as breathe, her hand gripping the door handle slowly.

The moment it clicked, Mr. Whisker's opened his eyes. Bella froze under the oddly judgmental stare of the cat. Slowly, she raised a finger to her lips. Mr. Whiskers only watched her.

Deciding that she must have received the approval of the cat, Bella slipped out of the drawing room. She closed the door quietly, then released her pent-up breath. A victorious grin stretched across her face. Bella backed away gingerly then turned and raced up the staircase to her bedchamber.

Her lady's maid, Annie, was already within, dusting. She dropped her rag in alarm the moment Bella burst through the door.

"Quick, Annie!" Bella gushed. "We haven't much time!"

"Much time for what, milady?" Annie asked hurriedly. Bella heard her approach her from behind but she was too busy rummaging through her armoire for her gloves. "Lady Isabella, is something wrong?"

"Not at all, my dear, Annie! Unless you consider my aunt falling asleep while I was under her watch something wrong." Bella whirled to face her, holding up a pair of blue gloves. "Do these match my dress?"

A confused frown fell over Annie's face. "I don't—I'm not certain—"

"Perhaps not." Bella tossed them aside, not caring where they landed. She snatched another. A pale-yellow pair, much better suited for her ivory-colored dress. "Quickly, Annie, find me a parasol and a bonnet."

"Are you going somewhere, milady?" Annie asked, still bemused. Even so, she got into action, claiming the task of rummaging through the armoire when Bella stepped away to tug on her gloves.

Gloves on, Bella made her way to her vanity table. Her hair was still in place, she saw, a simple chignon that held most of her blond hair at bay. If she were caught outdoors with a single strand of hair out of place, her father and Aunt Gertrude would know about it.

Not that she planned on getting caught. No, she had to return before her aunt woke. But for now, she needed to get out of here as quickly as she could.

"Yes, Annie," Bella answered, unable to keep the excitement from her voice. "I have decided to visit the British Museum."

Annie approached her with a bonnet and parasol in hand, her eyes wide with horror. "Alone, milady?"

"Of course not," Bella laughed. "Father will be the first to hear of such a thing and I'd rather not incur his wrath when I can avoid it. He will be home late, as he usually is, and I would have returned long before then."

"Does Lady Wentworth know of this, milady?"

Bella shook her head slightly, then allowed Annie to secure her bonnet. "She is napping in the drawing room. I wish to take advantage of the time I have." Bella caught the look on Annie's face and added, "There is no use trying to talk me out of it, Annie.

I've already decided to go and there is no changing my mind. And you will be accompanying me."

"Lady Wentworth will not like this," Annie expressed fearfully. "His Grace will be furious."

"All accurate presumptions, Annie. But you forget one thing."

"What's that, milady?"

Bella gave her a broad, mischievous grin. "I am my father's daughter."

Annie's shoulders sagged with defeat. There was no arguing with that. The Duke of Redshire was a notoriously stubborn man. That was the only trait Bella had inherited from him.

Parasol in hand, bonnet secured, Bella hurried out of the room with a reluctant Annie on her heels. She knew her lady's maid would not hesitate to accompany her. It went beyond simple duty. Annie had been her lady's maid for over five years now and had become her friend during that time, though Annie would never admit such a thing out loud. She would never allow Bella to head into trouble by herself.

It didn't take long for a carriage to be ready for their departure. Annie made a few more attempts to dissuade her of her foolhardy plan but Bella ignored her. She'd been vying to visit the museum since she set foot in London, the only good thing about coming here. Her mother had even gifted her tickets to be used whenever she wished. She wasn't about to let this opportunity slip through her fingers.

Do not go anywhere without your aunt.

Her father's warning echoed in her mind as their carriage rattled across the cobbled street. He had all but ignored her these past four years. Surely it wouldn't be so bad to ignore him this once?

Chapter One

"A break? You wish to take a break?"

Edward almost rolled his eyes at his father's incredulous tone. Instead, he rose and ambled over to the sideboard, pouring himself his third glass of whiskey for the afternoon. He wasn't one to indulge, but after spending nearly the entire morning in a meeting with his father, Edward wasn't certain he'd be able to manage much longer without the liquor easing his tense mind.

"Is that so difficult to imagine, Father?" Edward said, taking a small sip of his whiskey. He met his father's dark eyes from across the study. "We have been at this for hours and we are no closer to a breakthrough than when we first began. Surely you understand that taking a break may help."

"Do not take that tone with me, boy! I see no value in that foolish suggestion. Let us continue." Lord Humphrey Harrington, the Earl of Harenwood, was a predictable man at times. Edward could have recited those words at the exact same time if he'd dared to. He didn't know why he'd even made the suggestion in the first place.

Perhaps he was too tired, so mentally exhausted that he could no longer mind his words around his harsh and temperamental father. It was only a matter of time before he snapped.

He said nothing, simply watching as Humphrey rounded the large redwood desk dominating the north of the study and sank into his armchair with a huff. Scattered across the desk's surface were invoices and letters from merchants in India, the current root of Humphrey's problems. He'd dragged Edward into a meeting late this morning to discuss how best to expand their influence in the tea industry. According to Humphrey—and Edward couldn't help but agree—the first step would be to monopolize the industry in England before expanding across the borders. And their biggest rival was Lord Henry Brown, the Marquess of Thanebridge. A man nearly as ruthless a businessman as Humphrey was.

Nearly.

Even so, the meeting they had secured with Lord Thanebridge required extensive preparations, according to Humphrey. Edward, on the other hand, didn't know how much longer he could endure this.

"Lord Thanebridge sits on the House of Lords," Humphrey continued. "His own influence extends past our industry and delves into construction and mining as well…"

Edward stopped listening. He knew all there was to know about Lord Thanebridge. He had done the research, had presented it all to his father even though he knew that it would not be deemed enough. Right now, they were going in circles and Edward could no longer pretend to focus.

He wandered over to the window, still sipping his whiskey, his father's voice a drone in the background.

It was a lovely afternoon. One that would be much better spent outdoors atop a horse, or perhaps in the gardens with a good book. Not discussing business affairs.

"Are you listening?" Humphrey snapped, banging his hand on the table.

Edward looked over his shoulder at his father. Once upon a time, the anger on his father's face would have frightened him into submission. But he was seven-and-twenty years old, a man with his own accomplishments. Though he would never care to admit it, Edward was partially the reason their business in the tea industry had become what it was. He didn't need to fear his father anymore.

But it didn't mean the resentment didn't linger.

"Today is the day, you know," Edward said calmly. Always calm, while Humphrey was a mass of unbridled rage.

Humphrey scowled at him. They looked so much alike that it bothered Edward at times. The same tall, athletic build. The same dark, wavy hair. The same striking blue eyes. Had his father left that constant scowl behind, perhaps he would even be deemed handsome.

"What are you talking about?" Humphrey grumbled. "We don't have time for this."

Edward faced the window again, but didn't see anything but that fated day fourteen years ago. "The day she left. Do you remember what happened or was it all nothing but a foolish inconvenience for you?"

"Oh, not this again." The frustration in Humphrey's voice was stark. "What is wrong with you? How will you inherit the earldom if you keep clinging to such petty sentimentality?"

"She is my mother!" Edward didn't shout. He stopped doing so long ago, when he'd vowed to be nothing like his father. But that didn't mean the anger in his voice did not stand out.

"*Was.* She was your mother. And now, where is she, Edward?" Humphrey paused, as if he truly wanted a response to his question. "Dead. Gone from this world. Rather than lament on what we cannot change about the past, we need to focus on creating a future for ourselves."

"A future that includes dominating everything you touch," Edward said bitterly.

"Yes. Now let us continue."

And that was that. No apologies. No explanations. Nothing. After fourteen years, Humphrey still didn't deem it worthy.

Edward couldn't stay here any longer. He set his glass down and headed for the door. "I think you can handle this all on your own, Father."

"Edward, don't you set foot—"

He closed the door on his father's sentence. Edward stalked down the hallway, barking an order at the butler to fetch his coat and have a carriage prepared. With every step away from the study, his mood grew fouler, annoyed with himself for allowing his father to get under his skin like that. Edward had long since perfected the art of dealing with his father's cold nature, but a day like this had those raw memories pulling at the emotions he'd tried to keep locked away for years.

He would never forget the day she walked through the door, her screams still echoing throughout the hallways. The manor had been so big back then, even as he began to grow into himself at the age of ten-and-three. But when his mother walked out the door, driven away by a heated argument she had with Humphrey, the walls seemed even further apart.

Ten days. The late Countess of Harenwood had been away from home for ten days, staying with her sister in Bath as she calmed down. To this day, Edward still didn't know the nature of the argument, only that it had driven his fierce, beautiful mother out of the manor. On the tenth day, when she'd decided to return, a fever claimed her life.

It was a swift death, Edward had been told. She fell ill in the morning and the fever stole her breath by nightfall. Physicians assumed it was because of her fragile mental state, being away from home and the distress of her marriage, that caused her body to give up so quickly. Edward didn't care. All he knew was that his mother was gone and his father continued with his life as if nothing had happened.

The anger and resentment he had been choking down for years came back up like burning bile in his throat. He didn't have to wait long for his carriage and winced inwardly when he snapped at the coachman to take him to the museum. It was the only place he could think to go. Though he had inherited his father's appearance, his mother's love for literature and history was forever ingrained in him. He wanted to be surrounded by the things that reminded him of her.

Before long, the carriage pulled to a stop in front of the British Museum. He was inside within seconds, having visited so often that he had no need to procure tickets any longer. Inside, his angry steps slowed and he shoved his hands into the pockets of his coat. He let the rage simmer, walking without aim.

It wasn't particularly busy today, which gave him some relief. When the London Season was in full swing, these hallways would be swarming with people. For now, only a few milled about, the people growing sparser when he delved into a room that housed the Egyptian exhibits.

"Please stop fidgeting, Annie. You are distracting me."

Edward slowed, his eyes falling on a particular piece his mother had loved. It was only a collection of cracked vases and back then, Edward couldn't understand her fascination with them.

"You can tell they were made with love and care," she would say to him. "Much attention was put into creating these."

Since she was an avid lover of art as well, he'd trusted her word on that.

"Milady, I think it is best that we leave now," came a timid voice, breaking into Edward's reminiscing. "Surely Lady Wentworth has woken from her nap."

"It has only been a little more than an hour, Annie," the calm voice of a lady nearby stated. "My aunt will sleep for another hour. And don't forget that Father will be home late, so I have plenty of time."

"What if His Grace returns early this evening?"

"He won't," she stated confidently.

Edward couldn't concentrate. He wandered away from the vases to admire a set of hieroglyphics instead.

The voices followed.

"Don't you have any faith in me, Annie?" came the voice again, light with humor. It was closer now. "I have snuck out away from home many times before and I have never been caught."

"That was when we were in the countryside, milady. With the London Season upon us, His Grace will only become stricter. I do not think it is wise to invite his ire."

"I won't," she chirped. "Because he simply will not know."

Edward turned, intended to go the other way as to give the two women their privacy—and himself some peace of mind. Just as he did, he bumped into a small body with enough force that she seized his arm to steady herself.

"Forgive me," he said quickly. Without thinking, he put a hand on her elbow to make sure she did not topple over. His gaze fell to a pair of deep, emerald eyes.

Large eyes. Ones he could feel himself falling into, forgetting where and who he was. For a moment, they simply stared at each other, her small, pink lips parting in surprise.

But then she jerked away from him and Edward took in the rest of her.

She was indeed small. He towered over her tiny frame and yet she pulled her shoulders back and met his eyes as if she were twice his size. Hair like spun gold curled at her temples, the rest tucked into a thick knot at the nape of her neck. Her cheeks were flushed, her skin like alabaster.

"What were you doing around there?"

It took Edward a moment to realize that she had asked the question, her tone dripping with accusation.

"Pardon me?" he asked, bemused.

She narrowed her beautiful eyes at him. "You seemed awfully close. Were you spying on me? Eavesdropping on my conversation?"

The spell she had inadvertently cast on him was broken instantly. Edward lifted a brow. "And who might you be? You ask me such a thing as if I should know you. Or care about who you are."

"If you were not then perhaps, I was mistaken," she said stiffly. "Though I find it quite odd that you were standing so close to us."

"And I find it awfully odd that a lady of your obvious standing is here without a chaperone," Edward shot back. He couldn't help himself. The defiance packed into this small person was enough to intrigue him, rather than anger him.

"My chaperone is right here," she stated, slinging her arm through the cowering lady's maid beside her.

"Hm." Edward hardly spared the maid a glance. "Would that be enough for your slumbering aunt, I wonder?"

The lady's eyes went wide. "You were eavesdropping!"

"You were simply speaking too loudly. Tell me, Miss, do you make it a habit of picking a fight with strangers?"

Anger flared in her eyes. Edward fought his smile. He could see a battle waging within her, as if she was contemplating whether she should respond or not. He wished that she would.

But then her maid tugged on her arm and whispered something in her ear. Whatever it was must have been enough to calm her, somewhat.

The lady drew in a slow breath as if preparing herself for something. "You are right. Forgive me."

"You sound quite sincere," Edward drawled sarcastically.

She narrowed her eyes at him. "I do not care if you doubt my sincerity. I have apologised and now I shall take my leave. Please do not wander about this museum spying on other people, sir."

With that, she turned and walked away. Edward watched her go until she was out of sight, humor tugging at his lips. How hilarious of her to apologize for her accusations in one breath and then accuse him again in the other. He wondered how his mother would have reacted to an encounter like this.

Somehow, he got the feeling the late countess would have liked her.

Chapter Two

Bella's hands were still shaking. She gripped Annie's arm a little too tightly as they hurried to the carriage. The stranger's mirth-filled eyes lingered in her mind a little too long.

"Do you know who that was, milady?" Annie asked her once they were in the safety of the carriage.

Bella shook her head. She watched as the imposing building disappeared as the carriage pulled away. "No, I don't. At least, I do not think that I do. In hindsight, perhaps I should not have snapped at him the way that I did."

"Why did you?" Annie asked softly, clearly uncertain of whether she was passing her place by voicing such a question.

Bella sighed, burying her hands in her face. She was already ashamed of the entire interaction. That was not the impression she liked to make on strangers, but he had frightened her so much that she'd lashed out without thinking. "He reminded me too much of Lord Harold."

"The second son of the Earl of Kenton?"

"Yes, the same. Do you recall how he hounded me while we courted? And the way he would report my every move to my father hoping that it would bring his favour? It was clear that he would stop at nothing to secure a marriage, even though he'd quickly made it clear that he only wanted my dowry and not me."

"Oh, I see."

Except, Annie did not understand. She couldn't. When Bella had told Annie that she intended to sever her relationship with the lord, she had been appalled. He was handsome, attentive, and might have made a decent heir to her father's dukedom.

But Bella saw him for the overly ambitious man that he truly was. She couldn't stomach the thought of attaching herself to a man like him.

He hadn't been the only one. From the day she turned ten-and-seven, gentlemen all but lined up to ask for her hand in marriage. She'd given them all chances, hoping that the next suitor would be someone who truly cared for her. But they'd all shown themselves to be egotistical, power-loving men who only wanted power and wealth.

Why did that man remind her so much of Lord Harold?

She had reason to be cautious, she knew. Especially since she hadn't expected to come across anyone in such close quarters. What if he knew her father and intended to use this as blackmail to get closer to her? It had certainly happened before.

Even so, her reaction had been entirely rude and she was ashamed to have ended it that way. She hoped she never had to see him again.

Despite that, his striking blue eyes lingered in her mind all the way home.

The moment the carriage pulled into the driveway, Bella sensed that something was amiss. There was another carriage in the driveway as well, bearing the crest of her father's dukedom. Surely he hadn't returned home so early? He rarely came home before dinner and it wasn't even night yet!

Annie lingered behind as they made their way up to the front door. Whatever stood on the other side, it was clear she did not want to be in the line of fire. Bella wished she could turn back herself.

Please don't be on the other end, she silently prayed.

The moment she opened the door, her father's hard glare greeted her.

"Good evening, Father," Bella chirped, her heart fluttering with fear. "I did not expect you home so early."

"Is that why you thought to sneak out of the house like a rat?" Lord Victor Redcliffe, the Duke of Redshire, would not spare her, she knew. With his legs apart, his arms crossed, and that glare capable of turning the hardest man into a bumbling mess fixed on her, Bella knew there was no chance of talking herself out of it.

But she was nothing if not hopeful. "I know how this must look but—"

"How this must look?" he barked. "You are smarter than that, Isabella. How this looks is the only thing that matters! You were out in London without a chaperone doing who knows what!

Now when your disobedience reflects poorly on this family, what will you do?"

Bella tried not to hang her head in shame. He always had a way of making her feel as if she was nothing more than the dirt under his shoe. A constant disappointment that could not be fixed. No wonder he was so eager to marry her off lately.

"Father, I was careful," Bella carefully explained. "And I brought a chaperone. My maid was with me."

"Your maid," Victor spat. Bella saw Annie flinched in the corner of her eye. "What good will that do you? Didn't I tell you not to go anywhere without your aunt? She is an upstanding lady in London society and you have proven time and again that you are incapable of conducting yourself properly when left alone."

Bella thought of the way she'd snapped at the stranger at the museum and winced. "I understand, Father. But I only wished for a bit of freedom—"

"You argue too much, child!" he bellowed, his voice reverberating within the foyer. "You should know when to simply stop talking! I shall hear no more of your foolish excuses. Go to your chambers and you shall remain there for the rest of the night." He paused. Bella held her breath. "As a matter of fact, you shan't leave this manor unless I deem it fit."

"But, Father," Bella began, despite the voice in the back of her head telling her to just be quiet, "the Season has begun. Shall I remain out of the public's eye the entire time?"

"That is the price of your disobedience." He waved a dismissive hand, stalking away. "Now go. I am done with you."

Bella stared after him, then listened to the sound of his footsteps long after he was out of sight. Annie was still a quiet presence next to her, not daring to speak. Without another word, she made her way to her bedchamber, closed the door, and then sank to the floor to cry.

***

The hum of chatter reverberating throughout White's Gentleman's Club was usually a welcomed sound to soothe Edward's troubled mind. But this evening was different. He gazed out the window, an untouched glass of brandy in one hand. He came here because he didn't want to return home just yet and he hadn't been able to stop thinking about the lady at the museum.

"You'd better have a good reason for pulling me away from my training."

A disheveled man sank into the chair across from Edward, raking his fingers through his already unruly brown strands. Edward wordlessly slid the decanter of brandy towards his friend. Lord Luke Bentley, the Viscount of Fellington, waved a dismissive hand. Edward left it there. His friend would be reaching for it soon enough.

"Isn't loneliness and longing for company enough?" Edward drawled, reclining in his chair. He took in his friend's frazzled appearance, as if he had rushed in getting dressed. "It has been so long since we have shared each other's company, don't you think?"

"Out with it, Edward. Have you fought with your father again?"

Edward masked his instant scowl by sipping his brandy.

Luke grinned. He'd always had an easy demanour, from the way he spoke to the boyish appearance he hadn't quite grown out of. Even in the dim lighting of the club, his freckles stood out, his green eyes alight with humor.

"I'm right, aren't I? He's the only one capable of putting you in such a dour mood."

"I'm not in a dour mood," Edward grumbled and winced when he heard how much his tone contradicted his words.

"Yes, yes, so you say. What did he say this time? Did he pressure you again to marry? Or perhaps he has gotten more creative and has thrown a hapless young maiden in your path for you to take as your bride."

"Jest all you wish, Luke. It is only a matter of time before you will have to take a wife yourself. Your title requires an heir, after all."

"You and I both know that I have quite some time before I need to worry about that. You, on the other hand…"

Edward sighed. He didn't want to have this conversation. He'd spent the past few months dodging his father's attempts to get him married, distracting him as best as he could with business matters. But Luke was right. While his carefree friend still had years of bachelorhood ahead of him, Edward could feel the noose slowly tightening around his neck.

He didn't mind the idea of marriage. He understood the logical reasoning behind it, understood that it was proper to marry first then have an heir later. Edward had never clung to the silly notion that he should fall in love with his future wife.

But that didn't mean he wanted his father arranging a marriage that would only be means to strengthen his power and influence. Edward had no intentions of starting a family as a business transaction.

It had been a while since Humphrey had mentioned marriage to him. Edward knew better than to think that his father had decided to leave him alone.

"You're right," he confessed at last. "I could not stomach being in his presence any longer and so I left for the museum. To take my mind off things."

"Ah. Today is the day then?" Luke didn't really need to ask. He was Edward's closest friend. He knew how many scars had been sliced into Edward's heart the day his mother walked through that door.

"It reminds of me of her," Edward went on, staring unseeingly into his untouched glass. "Today more than ever. Though my time was rudely interrupted by a feisty, blond lady."

"Feisty, blond ladies." Luke grinned. "They have always been my favourite."

"I doubt this lady would have put that smile on your face. She attacked me out of nowhere." At the look of horror that crept over Luke's face, Edward chuckled. "Not physically, no. She accused me of eavesdropping on her conversation."

"Were you?"

"Not intentionally. Though, I must say, I found it rather interesting. It seems she left her home without permission."

"To go to the museum?" Luke wrinkled his nose in distaste. "I'm sure there are far more interesting places to go if one were to sneak out."

"I suppose there is something to be said about a lady that eager to partake in world history." Edward thought back on her blazing green eyes, so large they threatened to take over her face. A smile touched his lips. "Perhaps there is more to her than meets the eye."

Silence met his words. It took Edward a moment to realize that Luke was only staring at him. He frowned. "What is it?"

Wonder filled Luke's eyes, a mischievous grin lifting his lips. "You are smitten with her."

Edward scoffed. "She is a stranger."

"A stranger who has you grinning to yourself like a madman."

Edward poured him the glass of brandy and placed it directly. "Have a drink and be quiet."

Luke's laughter echoed throughout the club, earning a few curious glances. Edward tried not to laugh, not wanting to encourage him. Once Luke got something in his mind, it would be hard to convince him of otherwise.

Smitten? Edward couldn't recall ever feeling such a thing. He didn't pay the opposite sex much mind save for the barest of polite greetings. Many ladies were simply shells of their upbringings and lessons, with carefully crafted words with no meaning between them and hobbies with no passion. Echoes of their mothers, their aunts, and the countless other ladies who bury themselves under the guise of who a 'proper' lady should be.

No one had ever snapped at him like that, save for his father. Edward supposed that counted for something.

Chapter Three

The tentative knock on the door of Bella's chambers had her springing out of bed. Her hair tumbled down her back, a chill racing through her body the moment her feet touched the floor. Her heart began to race, even though she knew the person she wished to see the least might be on the other end.

I don't care. I'll do anything to get out of this room.

But only Annie stood on the other end, wearing a pitiful look. Bella was tired of seeing that face. It was the only expression she'd gotten from her maid ever since she was banned to her chambers three days ago.

Three days of being trapped within her bedchamber. Three days of taking her meals in bed or on her balcony, alone. Three days waiting for her father to lift his punishment, only to be met with stark disappointment.

Bella didn't bother holding back her sigh. "I am in no mood to eat, Annie," she declared, dragging herself back to the bed. She flopped on top with another heavy sigh.

"I come bearing good news, milady," Annie said from behind, closing the door behind her.

Bella sprang back up. "Has Father decided to lift my punishment?" she asked eagerly.

Annie shook her head sadly. Disappointment descended like a wave onto Bella's shoulders. "What good news could it possibly be then?"

A glimmer of a smile touched Annie's lips. "His Grace has requested your presence at breakfast. He says you must be ready within the hour."

Bella only looked at her. Silence stretched on, until Annie frowned in confusion. "Are you not pleased, milady?"

"I'm not certain," Bella admitted, nibbling on her bottom lip. "On the one hand, I will finally leave the confines of my chambers. On the other, I will have to face Father again."

"Perhaps he has forgiven you, milady."

Bella stood, shaking her head. She sat before her vanity table, frowning at her reflection. "I doubt it. He is not known to be a very forgiving man."

The thought of sitting next to her father after what she'd done unsettled her. The duke was a terrifying man. His presence alone had not been enough to scare Bella into submission. Knowing that he was angry with her was something else entirely.

His orders were not to be ignored, however. And this was exactly what this was. An order, not an invitation.

Annie fell into the practice routine of preparing Bella's clothing, pulling a lovely blue morning gown that was sure to impress the duke. She tried to engage Bella in lighthearted conversation. Bella tried to partake but found herself growing more anxious as the hour counted down to seconds. As she did her hair, got dressed, and dabbed a bit of rouge on her lips and cheeks, Bella began to dread the moment she would leave this room.

How amusing, she thought, *that I had been eager to leave just a short while ago.*

Soon enough, she left her chambers, Annie slipping off elsewhere. Alone, she hurried to the dining room, despite her nervousness. She wouldn't dare to keep her father waiting.

Her father and aunt were already seated. Bella's heart hammered madly against her chest, wondering if she might have miscalculated the time and had actually arrived late. The duke didn't look up at her arrival, but Gertrude glanced up with a look of empathy. Dread whispered through Bella at the sight.

"Good morning," Bella greeted softly as her chair was pulled out by a footman. Mr. Whiskers shot out from under the table all of a sudden. Bella jolted, her hip colliding into the table. The cutlery rattled atop plates.

"Sit down, child!" her father barked, making her jump.

Bella hung her head, sliding into the chair. She shot the cat a baleful look, but he simply flicked his tail at her.

"How did you sleep, Bella?" her aunt asked from across the table.

"Well, Aunt Gertrude," Bella answered, grateful for the distraction. "And you?"

"Like a newborn babe," Gertrude said amiably. "I certainly could use another hour or two in bed but your father insisted that I join you this morning."

"I am grateful for it." And grateful for her attempt to make conversation. Perhaps she too remembered the days this dining hall had once been filled with laughter and chatter.

Bella could still see Christopher stumbling through the door, half-bent in laughter at a joke he'd told himself and would share with no one. She could see him planting a kiss on their mother's cheek, then sinking into the same chair Bella claimed now. Christopher had been the sunshine in everyone's life. His absence brought nothing but darkness and shadows.

Victor cleared his throat, leaning back in his chair. "There is a reason I wished for both of you to be present. This evening, the Earl of Harenwood and his family will be joining us for dinner."

Bella said nothing, glancing at her aunt. But she seemed just as surprised.

"I cannot express how important this meeting is," her father went on. "I shan't allow the slightest imperfection. Do you hear me, Isabella?"

Meeting, he'd said. A dinner, yet a meeting. Bella shouldn't be surprised that this wasn't a social affair.

She shouldn't be surprised. She didn't know the earl personally, but she'd certainly heard rumors. He was known to be a callous, wealthy businessman with considerable influence. Of course, her father was acquainted with him.

"Yes, Father," she answered dutifully.

"As a matter of fact," Victor turned to Gertrude, "accompany Isabella on a shopping excursion this afternoon. Choose a dress that will impress."

"If you wish, brother."

Bella sipped her tea. Hesitated. Second guessed what she was about to do. And then decided to ask anyway. "May I ask why we are dining with the earl and his family, Father?"

"No," he answered briskly. "You may not."

And that was that. Bella fixed her eyes on the toast before her, not too embarrassed by his curt dismissal. Was she mistaken, or did her father sound a little...pleased? Was he happy to host dinner this evening? He hadn't done such a thing before. At least, not without her mother present. The duchess was usually the person planning these events and yet...

Bella picked up her toast and took a bite, her appetite returning. Now she had something to look forward to this evening.

***

"My Lord, please wait."

Edward paused, turning to look over his shoulder at his butler hurrying to his side. He handed him a folded letter with the Harenwood seal emblazoned on top.

Edward didn't touch it. Simply looked at it then at his butler. "What is this?"

"It was delivered a short while ago, my lord, while you were getting ready."

"Leave it on my desk."

Edward turned to leave but his butler persisted, "The messenger boy expressed that it was urgent."

He sighed. His father thought everything was urgent. When he summoned someone, he believed they should drop what they were doing to attend to his orders. Edward considered ignoring it, just leaving it on the desk in his study until he was in a better frame of mind to deal with his father. But Edward knew the consequences of such a thing and he didn't want to deal with that.

He slung his fencing sword from his shoulder and handed it to his butler. He took the letter. "You may as well put this away then. I will not be needing it any longer."

"What shall I tell Lord Fellington, sir?"

"Tell him that my father has ruined my day once again." Luke would probably laugh at that. He always found the tense relationship between Edward and his father amusing, probably because it wasn't something he could relate to. Luke's father had passed two years ago but they had a wonderful relationship before his death.

"As you wish. I shall send for your valet." Nearly as quickly as he'd appeared, the butler was gone.

Edward looked down at his father's seal with a sense of dismay. It had been days since he'd stormed out of their meeting. Edward knew that it was only a matter of time before he would have to see him again. He just hoped that it would be a couple more days.

It seems I will have to go fencing with Luke another time.

Edward trudged up the stairs back up to his bedchamber. His valet was already waiting to help him out of his fencing uniform. Within half an hour, Edward was donned in a pair of black breeches, a white shirt, a black waistcoat, with dark boots. He didn't care to style his hair and hoped that his father wouldn't bother to lecture him about it. He wasn't in the mood for it.

A carriage was waiting outside his townhouse. Edward climbed in, rested his head on the back of the seat, and closed his eyes. He could already feel a megrim pinching him between his eyes in apprehension.

His father's butler held the door opened by the time he approached the door. Edward gave him a brisk nod as he stepped into the foyer.

"Edward!"

The chirpy voice at the top of the stairs instantly lifted Edward's spirits. His sister flew down the steps at a frightening speed.

"Slow down, Amelia," Edward warned, meeting her halfway through the foyer. She flung herself into him, wrapping her arms around his neck and planting a kiss on his cheek.

"Oh, Edward, it's been too long! When you were here last, you didn't even bother to wait until I returned home to see you."

"It is not my fault you are so popular," Edward said with a grin. He set her gently onto the floor. "You spent nearly the entire day with your friends."

"We have much to talk about," she explained with a pout. She was still his adorable sister, even though she was slowly growing into a young lady. In two years, she would be ready to debut.

Unlike so many other ladies her age, Amelia would have no issues making friends when she debuted. Edward always compared her to a hummingbird. Always flitting from one place to the next, never able to stay still. How she had managed to stay put as ladies' seminary in Bath for the past few years was beyond him.

"Yes, I'm sure we do," Edward agreed, even though he knew that Amelia would be doing most of the talking. "But for now, Father requests my presence."

"He does?" Amelia's face fell, brows knitting with worry. "Whatever for?"

Edward couldn't help but chuckle at the look on her face. "Why do you wish to know? Will you walk in there with me and defend my honour?"

"It depends on if your honour needs defending," Amelia stated firmly.

Edward placed a hand atop her head. "You needn't worry about your brother, Amelia. I should be the one defending you."

"Don't treat me like I am a child, Edward." Amelia pushed his hand away, trying to look fierce. She only succeeded in looking like an adorable puppy. "You know how Father can be."

"I know." Edward tried not to sigh, plastering a smile on his face. "Which is why I should not keep him waiting, if I can help it."

Amelia didn't let him go. She seized his arm, pressing another kiss on his cheek. "You know where to find me when you're finished," she said, chirpy once more.

"The gardens?" Edward asked. Amelia shook her head. "The parlour? Your chambers?"

"Edward!"

Laughter bubbled up his throat as he began to turn away. "I know, Amelia. I know."

Amelia's answering laughter followed him down the hallway. It was enough to put him in better spirits, though every step towards his father's study sent it plummeting once more. Dread coiled in his stomach. He paused at the door, hesitating to knock.

Edward had never considered himself a coward. But dealing with his father in any capacity required a level of strength and courage that took a moment to muster.

He knocked twice, then entered without waiting for a response. Humphrey stood by the hearth, staring into the crackling fire with his hands clasped behind his back. He didn't move at Edward's entrance, nor did he say a word.

Edward endured the silence for only a few seconds. "Father," he called, barely containing his annoyance.

"Sit down."

Edward stayed by the door, crossing his arms.

Humphrey extended the silence for another minute before he looked over his shoulder at Edward. He grumbled something under his breath and ambled over to his desk. He sank into the chair like a man twice his age, taking a moment to center himself before he faced Edward.

"I have arranged a marriage for you."

Edward only blinked at him. Surely he had misheard?

"A marriage," he repeated dumbly.

"Don't anger me, boy. I am in no mood for this." Humphrey rubbed his temples wearily. "The Duke of Redshire has extended a dinner invitation for us this evening. There you will meet his daughter, your betrothed."

"I am betrothed to no one," Edward snapped. "Surely you do not expect me to sit back and allow you to dictate who I marry."

"That is exactly what I expect. I sat by and waited for you to take the initiative and you have done nothing. Even when I have presented potential brides."

"Has it ever occurred to you that I do not want your involvement in my future marriage?"

"It matters not what you think. You will have to marry whether you like it or not. Better sooner than later."

"Father—"

Humphrey's lip curled with distaste. "Don't tell me you have adopted your mother's foolish notions of love. Goodness, that woman haunts us even after all these years."

"Enough," Edward hissed. He was already backing towards the door, his anger pounding in the back of his head. He had no intention of listening to any of this. "You're mad if you think I will go through with your foolhardy attempts yet again."

"Don't you dare walk through that door." Humphrey didn't shout, which was alarming by itself. When Edward looked back at him, the glower on his face was enough to make up for it tenfold. "Or else I will withhold your allowance."

A harsh laugh echoed across the room, devoid of mirth. "Try again, Father. That isn't enough to frighten me. Surely you do not think about the meagre funds you give me as your son when I have created a name for myself already. I am the Viscount of Belmont, Father. I do not need your wealth or your title."

"What of your sister, then?" Humphrey regarded him with cold eyes. "What of your aunt?"

Cold horror washed over Edward as he took in his father. Anger unlike anything he'd felt before threatened to choke him. He curled his trembling hand into a fist, breathing slowly through his nose as if that would be enough to stop him from doing or saying something stupid. So many things came to his mind, his tongue heavy with scalding words capable of reducing his father to nothing. And he wouldn't care. Humphrey deserved it.

But his sister didn't. His aunt didn't. Until Amelia married herself, she was dependent on their father. Edward was also limited in his power since he was not her legal guardian. And Aunt Catherine, Humphrey's sister, was no better. With no heir, no husband, and a rapidly reducing inheritance, his aunt would suffer without Humphrey's allowance.

A look of satisfaction passed over Humphrey's face. "I thought so," he stated smugly. "You should know your place."

Edward didn't dare say a word, knowing nothing good would come from his mouth if he opened it.

His father, however, didn't seem to care about Edward's lack of response. He reclined in his chair, drumming his fingers on the mahogany table. "Her name is Lady Isabella Redcliffe. During this evening's dinner, you are to get to know your betrothed."

"Does she know?" Edward pushed through gritted teeth.

"She does not. Her father intends to inform her of the arrangement after dinner. You'd do best to hold your tongue about it until then."

Great, he thought bitterly. *I must befriend this lady while she is left completely in the dark.*

"That is all you need to know," Humphrey continued. He stood, wandering back to the fire. "You may leave."

Edward was glad to. He needed to get away from him, needed space and air and any way to release the rage smoldering deep within him. If he wasn't careful, he might do something he would regret and jeopardize Amelia's future.

"Edward?" his father called just as he opened the door. "Make sure you're on time."

The soft click of the door was the only response the earl received.

Chapter Four

Bella wasn't the type of lady who felt anxious. She remembered when she first met Gertrude, and how confused she would be when the older woman complained about her nerves. Fear, she understood. She felt fearful of her father all the time. Apprehension, perhaps. The usual anxiety one might feel when meeting strangers—strangers she was meant to impress—was not something Bella felt.

She tried to muster that feeling as she stared at her front door. She strained her ears to pick up the sounds of the carriage pulling into the driveway. The crack of stones under the wheels, the soft snorts of the horses. Bella tried to imagine the men alighting from the carriage without assistance, while the coachman hurried to assist the ladies. When she focused on that, it made it a little easier ignoring her father's overbearing presence so close to her.

Going from hardly seeing him at all to seeing him twice in one day made her head spin. She chanced a glance at him. He stood tall, with his hands clasped behind his back. Chin cocked, Victor Redcliffe appeared every bit the Duke of Redshire, dashing and perfect from the slick of his hair to the shine of his boots.

Next to him stood her aunt, looking fashionable and proper in a primrose dinner gown. Buttons adorned the front of her dress all the way to her neck. Pearls were strung around her throat and a matching pair of earrings complemented her appearance. Unlike Bella, she had opted for a more complicated hairstyle, so many ringlets tucked on top of her head that Bella wondered how it wasn't driving her insane.

Licking her lips, Bella focused her attention on the door once more. She mimicked her aunt, clasping her hands in front of her. Her gloves were long, frilly things that she hated. Gertrude had insisted that her father would love it however, and Bella had to admit that it did match her gown. The dress clung to her soft curves, dipping elegantly at her bosom with sleeves that cupped her shoulders and lacing that wrapped the midsection. When she'd come down to the foyer, her father had looked her up and down, grunting something under his breath. The fact that he didn't send her back to her chambers told her that she passed his strict approvals.

Gertrude had outdone herself, of course. Not hindered by price, she'd dragged Bella to Bond Street and had refused to leave until they had a new dress and a new pair of gloves. After returning home, Bella had spent the rest of her day with the modiste to ensure that the dress fit her perfectly. By the time that was over, it was time to get ready.

Needless to say, she was exhausted and starving.

How long does it take someone to walk from their carriage to the front door?

As soon as the thought crossed her mind, the butler approached the door. Bella straightened, not missing the moment her aunt held her breath. She couldn't understand why. They'd entertained many others at dinner before, though usually under her mother's watchful eye. Even so, what made this one so different?

She would ask her aunt about it later, she decided. For now, she plastered a smile on her face.

The butler opened the door, revealing a burly man first. He was stocky with a receding hairline and hard eyes. He brushed into the foyer as if he'd been here a thousand times before, making a beeline for Victor. The broad grin on his face did nothing to hide his frightening demeanor.

"Victor!" he greeted, his voice booming through the foyer. "What a procession! You would think I am the Prince Regent himself!"

"Perhaps you are not," her father responded with a—Bella could hardly believe her eyes—broad smile. "But you may as well be, my friend. Welcome to my residence. Allow me to introduce you to my family."

Victor gestured to Gertrude, who sank into a curtsy the moment the earl's eyes were on her. "This is my sister, Lady Gertrude. And this," he gestured to Bella, "is my daughter."

"Ah, Lady Isabella." The earl barely acknowledged Gertrude. He reached out a hand to Bella. She knew she had no choice but to take it. Her skin crawled when he placed a kiss on the back of it. "I have heard such lovely things about you. The apple of your father's eye, I've learned."

Bella didn't dare to let her smile slip, even though the only thing she wanted to do was pull her hand from his tight grip. "It is a pleasure meeting you, my lord."

"I'm sure," the earl purred, then finally moved away. Two ladies stepped forward. "Allow me to introduce my daughter, Lady Amelia and my sister, Lady Catherine."

Lady Amelia and Lady Catherine appeared as different as fire and water. Lady Amelia wore a bright smile, excitement dancing in her eyes. Even though she dipped into an elegant curtsy, the smile never left her face. She seemed genuinely happy when she said, "A pleasure."

Lady Catherine, on the other hand, looked as if she hadn't smiled in years. She didn't bother trying though her curtsy was every bit as proper as her niece's. "I agree," she said stiffly. When she straightened, Bella could have sworn she lifted her nose a little higher.

"And this," the earl continued, "is my son, Edward, the Viscount of Belmont."

Bella had been so focused on the earl and the two ladies that she hadn't focused on the other person who had entered. She turned to face him, offering him that same gentle smile her aunt had taught her.

The smile fell the moment she spotted a pair of striking blue eyes.

Surprise now shimmered in those eyes. For a moment, they only stared at each other. Bella wondered if he was reliving that moment at the British Museum like she was. If he was feeling the same amount of horror she did.

It couldn't be. The man she had so rudely shouted at was the son of the Earl of Harenwood? Oh, truly, this was sure to be a disaster.

Bella braced herself, clenching her jaw. He was going to reveal what happened between them, she knew. Oh, her father's fury might just keep her locked away for an entire month this time.

A smile touched his lips. Bella stiffened when he swept into a low bow. "It is a pleasure meeting you, my lady."

She blinked at him. "The pleasure is mine, sir," she murmured, unsure of what to do. Wasn't he going to tell everyone that they'd run into each other at the British Museum?

Bella remembered her manners half a beat later and quickly dipped into a curtsy. When she straightened, the gentleman was staring at her, that tiny smile on his lips.

"Now, shall we begin?" Victor announced with a clap of his hands. The earl and he were already turning away, clearly not caring about anyone else now that the introductions were over. Lady Amelia all but skipped behind them, Lady Catherine following along.

Bella knew she should move, but she couldn't look away from him. She hadn't realized he was this handsome, with black hair that curled at his neck and a sharp jaw dusted with the makings of a beard. He was the tallest man in the room. She was dwarfed by him and yet she didn't feel intimidated. She felt...

"Bella?" Gertrude's confused voice broke through her reverie.

Bella blinked, remembering where she was. And remembered how rude it was to stare. She flushed, looking at her aunt with an explanation on the tip of her tongue.

"Let us go," her aunt urged before she could say anything. Bella nodded, grateful that she needn't say anything. She didn't dare chance another glance at Lord Belmont, afraid that she could catch him looking again. Those eyes of his may be what kept her in a trance.

As she started behind her aunt, Mr. Whiskers appeared in the foyer. The moment Bella neared him, the temperamental cat hissed and swiped his claws at her. Bella barely managed to dodge it, rolling her eyes at him. She could never keep up with the cat. Just earlier he had been curled up in her bed, now he was acting as if he hated her.

Mr. Whiskers continued along, heading directly towards Edwards. Both Bella and Gertrude paused and looked at each other. Nothing good came from Mr. Whiskers interacting with strangers.

"Mr—"

"What a sweet cat," Lord Belmont murmured. He bent to pet Mr. Whiskers, who wound himself around the lord's legs and began to purr. "What is his name?"

"Mr...Mr. Whiskers," Bella murmured, shocked. Mr. Whiskers hated strangers. Bella was certain that the cat would have attacked him. Gertrude clearly had thought the same thing if the look of surprise on her face was any indication.

"He likes him," Gertrude whispered to Bella. "Surely that is a good sign?"

"Of what?" Bella whispered back.

"That he is a good man." Gertrude sounded delighted by that fact. She slid her arm through Bella's. "Come. We don't want your father waiting for long. My Lord?"

Lord Belmont seemed reluctant to leave the cat alone but he stood, meeting Bella's eyes once more. He didn't take them off her until he made it back to their side. Even when they made it to the dining hall, and parted ways, she could still feel the burning mark of his gaze.

***

She was utterly gorgeous. He had almost forgotten how viscerally the sight of her had taken his breath away the first time he saw her that the second time was nearly as crippling. Edward tried to take his eyes off her, knowing how uncomfortable he must be making her with his stares. But he couldn't. Lady Isabella was like a painting, every stroke, every curve, every line done with perfection.

She didn't look at him since they sat down to eat.

Edward couldn't blame her. After all, who would have thought that the same person who'd accused him of eavesdropping a few days ago would be the same person he was meant to marry. He shifted uncomfortably in his chair. It certainly didn't make things any better that she didn't know about it.

They were seated next to each other. Edward was sure that wasn't a coincidence. His father had made sure to remind him on their way there that his only duty was to befriend Lady Isabella. It certainly made things easier if they were sitting right next to each other.

He couldn't think of a single thing to say to her, though. Edward wasn't certain he really wanted to. Despite his father forcing his hand, he didn't want to roll over and let this happen so easily.

"It pleases me that we are finally able to get our family together," Victor said. The duke, Edward found, was just like his father. A resolute gentleman who adeptly feigned high social standing when necessary. This was exactly what he was doing. Putting on airs. Edward hadn't missed the sharp look he'd given his daughter while she'd faltered on her manners in the foyer.

"Yes, I must agree," Humphrey said with a nod. "It is such a pity that the rest of your family is not here to join us."

"You will meet them in due time," Victor chuckled. "Too many of us at once and I fear your son and daughter may become overwhelmed."

Humphrey laughed heartily at that. "I shall take your word for it."

Edward tuned them out. They didn't seem interested in involving anyone else in the conversation nor did he want to. He endeavoured instead to divert his attention from the presence of Lady Isabella by his side.

"My lord."

Edward nearly jumped at her whisper. He glanced down but her attention was on her meal. "Yes, my lady?"

"Why didn't you say anything?" she asked softly. She ate daintily, every bit the proper lady Edward was sure she was expected to be.

He didn't have to ask what she was referring to. "I didn't think it important to. Why? Would you like for me to say something now? Because I can—"

"No, of course not!" she said quickly. "I'm...just surprised, that's all. I was certain you would have told everyone about what I said to you."

"Why?"

"Because...well, I know I was not very nice to you."

"Oh, you *know*?" Edward couldn't help the note of amusement that slipped into his tone. From the way her grip tightened on her fork, she didn't appreciate it. "How odd that you know and yet I have not received an apology."

"If you intend to be so smug about it then perhaps, I shall not give you one."

"Very well." Edward cleared his throat. Lady Isabella sucked in a sharp breath.

"No," she whispered under her breath. He watched as her eyes darted to the head of the table, where the others were still engaged in conversation. "I'm sorry for how I attacked you, my lord. It shan't happen again."

"Why do I find that last part hard to believe?"

"The proper thing to say would be 'Apology accepted'."

"The proper thing would have been not accusing strangers the first time you meet them," Edward couldn't help but say. He didn't know why he was taunting her but he felt an odd shade of pleasure at the annoyed glare she shot him. The elegant lady he'd witnessed in the foyer was slowly devolving into the lady who had attacked him at the museum.

"Tell me, Lady Isabella," he murmured, leaning a little closer to her. "Do you visit the museum often?"

Isabella looked at him with incredulous eyes. "Why would you like to know that?"

"I am merely curious, my lady. Nothing more."

"Hm." She left it at that, not offering another word.

As the silence stretched on, punctuated by the occasional comment by Humphrey or Victor, Edward waited for something. When it was clear that Isabella had no intention of responding, he chuckled to himself.

"I suppose that says it all," he said, loud enough for her to hear.

Lady Isabella did not respond with anything save for a small nod. The conversation was over. This lady was not fond of him in the slightest. He couldn't help but wonder if that would change when she found out that they were to be wed.

He had a feeling it would only get worse.

Chapter Five

Bella was trying her best to ignore the handsome lord to her right and that, she admitted to herself, was the hardest thing she'd ever done. He exuded charisma that threatened to consume her. Every move he made, every word he spoke, left her spellbound, unable to do anything but focus entirely on him.

It was alarming since he didn't even say much. The majority of the dinner passed in comfortable conversations, spearheaded by Humphrey and Victor, punctuated now and again with Lady Amelia's eager questions. Bella tried and failed to keep up. She knew her father would have something to say about it later but for now, all she could do was try not to focus on the magnetizing man by her side.

Eventually, the final course was cleared away and the end of tonight's dinner loomed close. Bella felt a spark of regret at the fact that she'd barely participated. Lady Amelia had asked her a few questions but the moment she felt Edward's eyes on her, she faltered.

She never truly felt nervous before but this felt eerily similar to it.

"What a lovely dinner," Lady Catherine said once the dishes had all been cleared. Her tone was polite, but dry. "Thank you again, Your Grace, for your hospitality."

"It needn't end here," Victor said, preparing the state of what Bella had been dreading. "Humphrey, why don't we make our way to the parlour? I have a decanter of aged whiskey I have been itching to show you. Your son should join us."

"To display to my amusement, you mean." Humphrey laughed, a gravelly sound that grated Bella's ears. "Lead the way, my friend."

"While the men are occupied," Gertrude spoke up on cue, "why don't we ladies make our way to the drawing room? I'm sure Isabella would love to entertain us on the pianoforte."

"Aunt Gertrude…" Bella whispered but her aunt ignored her. Bella was never good at the pianoforte. She'd never done well with the arts overall. The last time she'd attempted watercolor painting, it had turned into a splotchy mess. Her aunt had taken one look at it and simply said, "Interesting."

Why would she have her sit and struggle at the pianoforte when she knew she was so terrible at it?

But there was no stopping it. The men were already coming to a stand. Bella felt a tug on her chair and looked up in surprise to see Lord Belmont holding on to her chair.

"Allow me, my lady," he said, his voice a deep rumble that shook her to her core.

"Thank you." Bella hastily rose to her feet and put three feet of distance between them. To her horror, she felt heat creeping over her cheeks. To make matters worse, the viscount looked at her like he knew exactly what was going on in her mind.

For a few seconds, they only stared at each other. And then someone seized Bella's arm. The smell of fresh citrus wafted over her.

"Would you like to play the pianoforte together, Lady Isabella?" Lady Amelia asked, her voice high with excitement.

"I, um—"

"I haven't played in a while," she went on. "I may not be very good right now, I'm afraid."

"Amelia, I'm sure Lady Isabella would like to do it on her own," Lord Belmont said, his tone patient.

I would much rather not do it at all, Bella wanted to say.

Amelia pouted. "Hurry along, Edward. Father and His Grace are waiting for you."

Sure enough, the duke and earl had already left the room, clearly not caring about anyone else.

"I just want to make sure you won't bother Lady Isabella," Lord Belmont said simply.

"I am never a bother." Lady Amelia huffed, pulling Bella closer to her. "Let us go, my lady. My brother will nag us to no end if we linger here any longer."

Lady Amelia didn't give her a chance to respond. Bella was whisked away, trailing behind Gertrude and Lady Catherine. She didn't dare to look back but she could almost feel the viscount's eyes following her as she left.

"Don't mind my brother," Lady Amelia said the moment they were out of the dining hall. Her grip on Bella's arm was nearly painful. "He can be such a busybody at times."

"Ah, I see," Bella murmured.

"He means well, though," Lady Amelia went on. "I'm sure he would much rather spend his time listening to your playing than talking with our fathers."

"Is that so?"

"What song will you play for us? Oh, goodness, had I known, perhaps I would have carried my harp with me."

Bella didn't bother to answer and Lady Amelia didn't seem to mind her silence. She chattered on in Bella's ear, talking about all the instruments she wished to learn before she grew old. Bella didn't mind the incessant talking. Lady Amelia's amiable personality made it easy for her to relax...a far cry from how tense she'd been sitting next to her brother.

Lady Catherine was already settled into Gertrude's favorite armchair by the time Bella entered the drawing room, her eyes narrowed at Mr. Whiskers who was watching her from across the room. Bella tried not to laugh at the disdain in the woman's eyes. Her mirth was quickly cut short when Gertrude said, "Come now, Bella. Don't make us wait long."

Reluctance trembled deep within Bella's core as she approached the pianoforte. It was sure to be horrible, she knew. Especially since she was doing it in front of company.

In a fit of desperation, Bella fixed her most charming smile on her face and said, "I am feeling a bit tired, Aunt. Perhaps—"

"I'm sure this will lift your energy a bit," her aunt said with a matching smile that told Bella everything she needed to know. *No arguments.*

With a soft sigh, Bella sat. She ran her fingers over the keys and tried to quell the trepidation. Then she began.

It wasn't horrible for the first few notes. She started slowly, an easy song that she hoped wouldn't be too difficult to do. But then her fingers fell short on a key and it went downhill from there.

Bella tried her best not to wince through the entire performance. As it drew to an end, she sped up her playing so that it could end quicker. Her finger banged on the last key and the sound echoed its way to silence.

And then hearty applause sounded behind her. Bella swiveled on the stool to see Lady Amelia clapping with exuberance, a broad grin on her face. "That was lovely, Lady Isabella! Absolutely lovely."

A kind lie. One that Bella didn't doubt that Lady Amelia believed, for some reason. She smiled and stood to curtsy. "Thank you. Thank you."

The pinched look on Lady Catherine's face told Bella that she didn't share in Lady Amelia's sentiment. "What an...interesting way of describing that performance, Amelia."

"Isabella is far more inclined towards literature," Gertrude explained. Bella didn't miss the look of resignation she gave her. "Her talents spread far, I assure you."

"If you say so." Bella didn't think it possible but Lady Catherine's managed to look down at Bella even though she was the one sitting. "Are you well versed in Shakespeare? Amelia has memorized his sonnets to near perfection, as if expected of her if she wishes to find a proper husband. Tell me, Lady Isabella, do you intend on getting married?"

Bella couldn't understand the question. Which lady didn't want to get married? It was as expected of her as the flowers were expected to bloom during springtime.

She mulled over the question for a moment, quelling the rise of annoyance she felt at Lady Catherine's words. There was no reason for a stranger to waltz into her home and question her like this. But her father's words rang in her ears. She had to make a good impression.

"That is my intention, my lady," Bella said after a moment.

"Then what do you have to show for it?" The lines around Lady Catherine's lips tightened. "A half-hearted attempt at the pianoforte? What will you do when—"

"I think it was lovely," Lady Amelia cut in. "Speaking of lovely things, has anyone gotten the chance to attend the theatre lately?"

Thankfully, the conversation slowly turned towards the theatre and other events to occur during the first half of the Season—much to Lady Catherine's reluctance. Lady Amelia and Gertrude bore the brunt of the conversations while the earl's sister sat stewing in her silence, huffing in annoyance now and again. Bella couldn't understand why she was being so unpleasant, but she was grateful that at least the attention was no longer on her.

She did want to be married, she decided. It would be nice to have someone to care for, to be loved, but in today's society that was a fading dream. Bella knew she was better off hoping that her future husband was at least kind. A man of her choosing.

Perhaps a man who made her feel as entranced as Lord Belmont.

***

"I must say, Your Grace, I am surprised that it took us this long to make this decision."

Edward watched the grin on his father's face with a glimmer of annoyance. He sat broodingly by the window with a glass of whiskey in his hand, gaze shifting from the earl to the duke and back.

He didn't think he would ever meet someone as terrible as his father.

The Duke of Redshire was Humphrey's match in nearly every way. Though they were physically different, the duke's large and commanding presence making the earl appear stunted, their mannerism was nearly identical. It was unnerving watching them speak as if no one else was around.

Edward didn't mind being ignored. He would sneak out of the room altogether if he thought that he could get away with it.

"My exact same sentiments," His Grace said. He was on his third glass of whiskey, his cheeks tinged pink in inebriation. "Though a sound decision made late is a sound decision all the same. At the rate my daughter was going, she would be a spinster by the end of the year."

"Edward is no better," Humphrey said. He pointed directly at Edward without looking at him and scoffed. "I have been trying to convince him to get married these past few years and he has done nothing but spit in my face like the ungrateful person he is."

"Isabella as well. She has had many suitors but deemed them all unworthy of her affections, clearly. It was only a matter of time before I could no longer give her the courtesy of choice."

Edward rolled his eyes, turning towards the window as he tuned them out. It came as no surprise to him that Lady Isabella had many suitors before. She was a beauty, after all. Any man with a good set of eyes and the barest sprinkle of common sense would be interested in the beautiful daughter of the Duke of Redshire.

But he couldn't help but wonder what made her lose her interest in them. Why hadn't a single one of them been deemed worthy of her time and affection? Edward thought of the way she snapped at him at the museum. Perhaps it had less to do with them and more to do with the fact that she was not the demure, polite lady that many gentlemen wished to have as their wives. Maybe they were the ones who lost interest in her?

He shook his head, sipping his whiskey. Nonsense. Lady Isabella was a well-esteemed and sought-after lady, as elegant and refined as any lady of her status. The brief interactions had already made that clear. So what was it?

Edward looked at the duke, who was now going on about the benefits merging their families would have. Every time he looked at him, the similarities between the duke and his father were uncanny. Lady Isabella hadn't seemed particularly afraid of her father, but the duke had hardly acknowledged her save for the standard introduction in the foyer. Edward could only imagine how things were behind closed doors.

And now she was meant to marry a man she hardly knew. They hadn't even deemed it necessary to inform her of the decision.

Pity whispered through him. This marriage was sure to happen. Edward couldn't fight it—not with Amelia and Catherine's futures being dangled before his face—and he didn't think Lady Isabella would fare any better. He had no power right now and neither did she.

The only thing he could do was make this marriage a good one. One that would work. One that didn't leave him with the constant reminder that he was no better than his father, who had driven his mother to her death.

Chapter Six

Sleep threatened to keep Bella within its warm, comforting embrace for a few hours longer. She would have given in to it had it not been for Gertrude's warning last night, just before Bella was about to retire for bed.

Make sure to have breakfast with us in the morning. Your father wishes to speak with you.

Bella didn't know how she even managed to sleep at all with the trembling fear of what her father would want to speak to her about. Fatigue weighed her down as she got ready. Annie was silent during the entire process though Bella did not miss the worried glances now and again. Bella couldn't muster the strength to engage in any conversation. Between needing to sleep and pair of icy-blue eyes following her into her dreams, Bella felt like half her normal self.

She dragged herself to the first floor and twisted her face into a pleasant expression before entering the breakfast room. To her immense relief, only Gertrude was on the other end. Mr. Whiskers sat purring in her lap, giving Bella a look of annoyance as she approached as if she was disturbing his private time.

"Good morning, Aunt," Bella greeted, not bothering to hide the tiredness in her voice. Perhaps after breakfast she could sneak back to her chambers and lay down for a nap. She need only get through the next hour or so.

"Have you slept?" her aunt asked with a crook of her brow. "You look horrid."

"Just the thing a lady wishes to hear first thing in the morning," Bella sighed. She reached for the pot of hot chocolate, wishing she could have the coffee instead. But she didn't dare to, knowing her father's thoughts on a lady drinking such a thing.

"It may not be what you want to hear but it is what you should hear." Gertrude made a show of looking Bella up and down, scrutinizing every inch of her. "You look well put together, despite your sunken eyes. Let us hope your father does not notice."

Bella reached for a toast, giving her aunt a curious glance. "Do you happen to know what he wishes to speak to me about?"

"You will know soon enough," Gertrude answered dismissively. She stroked Mr. Whiskers and he finally stopped glaring at Bella, settling back into a nap.

"Then where is he? Surely he must have woken by now?"

"Your father is a busy man, Bella. He has been up since dawn."

Bella wrinkled her nose. "After drinking so heavily last night? That hardly sounds like a healthy thing to do."

"Hush now," Gertrude shushed, though Bella could have sworn her aunt's eyes glimmered with humor. "We cannot begin to understand the work he does to keep this roof over our heads."

Bella nodded, deciding to leave it at that. When the time came for their guests to leave last night, Bella hadn't missed how inebriated her father had seemed. He stunk of whiskey, a grin quick to his lips, and his voice much louder than necessary. She hadn't noticed anything else however since she had been trying her best to ignore Lord Belmont and the rapid beating of her heart whenever he looked at her.

Before she could say anything, the door opened and her father strolled in. Bella held her breath, watching him as he stalked towards them and sank into the chair next to Gertrude. He didn't greet them, only reached for the coffee.

"Good morning, Father," Bella murmured. He looked perfectly put together as normal, but his night of drinking showed in the pallor of his skin.

Victor grunted something under his breath and then there was silence. The only sound that could be heard was the occasional clink of cutlery and the intermittent slurps Victor took of his coffee.

Then he broke the silence by saying, "Isabella, I have arranged a marriage for you."

Bella's teacup nearly slipped from her fingers. She caught herself in time, swallowing past the lump that had formed suddenly in her throat.

"Pardon?" she whispered.

Annoyance flickered in her father's eyes. "Do not make me repeat myself. You will be married to the Viscount of Belmont."

"Lord Harenwood's son?" Bella gasped. She knew it was a mistake as soon as she said it but she couldn't help herself. She should have known that there was more to last night's dinner. Bella had just assumed that her father wished to strengthen business relations with the earl but he'd never cared to involve her before. This time, he wanted *her* to make a good impression. And now she knew why.

"It is about time," her father went on, continuing to eat as if they were having a casual conversation about the weather and not her future. "Any longer and you will be deemed unmarriageable. I thought to take matters into my own hands."

"I cannot," Bella blurted out. Both Victor and Gertrude looked sharply at her. "Father, I cannot marry a man I do not know."

"Isabella…" her aunt murmured in a warning tone. Bella ignored her.

Victor leaned back in his chair, regarding her evenly. "Then what would you like to do instead, Isabella? After two years you have failed to secure a single match, so what will change now?"

"Give me some more time," Bella begged. Desperation tinged her voice but she didn't care. "This Season I will—"

"Two years, Isabella!" Her father's bellow made her flinch. Redness washed his face in his sudden anger. "I have given you two years and you have done nothing with the time! Not to mention your actions and your behaviour will only lead you to trouble that I will not be able to fix one day. You are one bad decision away from a scandal, Isabella, and then you will be worth nothing to me."

The lump was now threatening to stop her breathing altogether. Bella tried to hold herself together, to focus on the anger his words stirred rather than the hurt. Even as tears stung the back of her eyes, she told herself it was her rage.

"Is that all I am to you?" she whispered. She didn't have the strength to shout like he did but he heard her all the same. "Just a pawn to be used that will benefit you?"

"You are to be married to the Viscount of Belmont and that is that. I will hear no more of your protests about the matter. It has already been decided."

Bella wanted to argue with him. She wanted to scream and shout and cry until he understood what he was doing to her. But the man sitting across from her would only throw up another icy wall between them. So many of those stood there now and Bella had barely been able to chip away at a single one. She stood no chance with another.

She remembered a time when her father once laughed easily. When he could come down for breakfast and kiss his wife on the temple, would engage in whatever hearty discussion was happening at the table.

That was the man her father had been before Christopher's death. The man he was now was a stranger.

Bella struggled to think of what to say as her father got to his feet. He didn't say anything when he stalked away but Mr. Whiskers didn't like being disturbed once more. He hissed and swiped his nails at Victor, missing him by a hair as the duke left the room. To Bella's surprise, Gertrude chuckled under her breath.

Bella turned her watery eyes to her aunt. "Did you know?"

Gertrude looked at her with shades of pity and shame. She said nothing straight away, focusing on calming her cat instead. Her silence said it all.

Too many words rushed to Bella's mind, too many feelings piling atop each other. Too many for her to handle all at once. She stood, hands curled into fists. Before the first tear fell, she was out the door. By the time Bella made it to her bed, there was no holding them back any longer.

***

"Well, you look horrible."

Edward grunted something unintelligible under his breath. Luke chuckled but said no more, opening the copy of the Times instead. Steaming coffee sat on the table before them and he poured himself a glass with the newspaper resting on his lap.

Edward had been the one to call him to the club. He didn't usually spend mornings here, but between barely being able to sleep last night and the pressing need to get all the weight off his chest, Edward needed an outlet.

Now that Luke was here, however, he realized that he wasn't ready to speak. Not yet. He was still so angry, too angry to do anything but stew in it. He kept thinking about everything that had happened last night, how he had been pulled along like a puppet on a string unable to do anything. Edward had decided a long time ago that he would never give his father power over him and yet here he was. Succumbing to his will.

He finished an entire cup of coffee and was about to reach for his second when Luke gave up on maintaining the quiet. Luke set the newspaper aside and fixed Edward with a worried look.

"All right, out with it. Why have you been sighing to yourself this whole time?"

"Have I?" Edward hadn't noticed.

"What has your father done now?" Luke paused, then leaned forward with a grin. "Or does this have anything to do with your new belle from the museum?"

Edward winced, pinching the bridge of his nose. Luke's grin fell.

"Do not tell me that I am right?" he asked, eyes wide.

"I wish it weren't so either," Edward admitted. "A complete coincidence, I assure you, though I cannot help but wonder what odd twist of fate could have created a situation like this. Father wishes for me to marry her, you see."

"But..." Luke's frown grew deeper. "I'm afraid I do not understand."

"She is the daughter of the Duke of Redshire," Edward explained, his tone a little more bitter than he meant it to be. "And they have decided that we are to be wed. Apparently, she seems no more interested in securing a match as I am and her father has grown tired of it. I'm sure you have imagined the benefits my father will receive from such a union. He does nothing if he sees no advantage in it."

Luke still looked confused. "That I can imagine. Lord Harenwood is a self-serving man, through and through. But what I don't understand is why you seem so bothered by this. This isn't the first time your father has tried to secure a match for you and you've always thwarted his attempts."

"That is because he has decided to neglect both Amelia and Aunt Catherine if I do not comply." Saying it aloud brought the anger back with full force. Edward drummed his fingers on the table in front of him in the hopes that it would relieve some of the ever-present fury.

Luke said nothing. For the first time, it seemed he was shocked into silence. Edward couldn't blame him. He was as fond of Amelia as Edward was, seeing her as the sister he'd never had. To know that her future was being threatened just to get Edward to conform to Humphrey's plans really did upset him as well.

"What shall you do?" Luke asked after the long moment of silence.

"You know very well what I intend to do."

Luke nodded. There was no need to clarify. "Then you have my support. No matter what."

Edward nodded his thanks. Luke understood him, he knew. Even if he couldn't relate, he understood and that was what mattered right now. It helped Edward a little to know that, at the very least, he did not have to go through this alone.

He only hoped that Lady Isabella could say the same.

Chapter Seven

"Have a seat, Bella."

Bella did so reluctantly. She knew she was not a good sight. She'd spent half the morning crying and the evidence of such shown in the redness of her cheeks. Gertrude didn't like it when a lady wasn't put together at all times.

But now, Gertrude said nothing. She simply watched Bella as she sat in the chaise lounge across from her. Bella braced herself for whatever banal task her aunt was going to give her. If it had anything to do with Shakespeare, Bella had little confidence that she wouldn't start crying again. If it involved the pianoforte, she intended to feign sickness and leave altogether.

"I wished to speak with you," Gertrude said instead. Of course, Mr. Whiskers was right by her side, belly splayed to the ceiling as he slept soundly.

Bella blinked. She'd been almost certain that her aunt would subject her to Shakespeare again. "About what?"

"Your impending marriage." Gertrude said matter of factly, but her tone held a note of sympathy. "To answer your earlier question, I did know. Your father informed me of it yesterday morning."

"Why didn't you tell me?" Bella asked before she could stop herself. "You could have warned me."

"What good would that have done? He'd already made up his mind and you know better than I that there is no changing it. In any case, he told me not to say anything to you."

Bella thinned her lips, hands curling into fists in her lap. "Well then, there is nothing for us to talk about then, is there?"

Gertrude shook her head patiently. "My marriage was an arranged one as well. Did you know that?"

"I...did not."

"I was young. Ten-and-seven. I had debuted only a few weeks prior to the arrangement and so I did not get the chance to be courted by any gentlemen. At the time, I resented the marriage as much as you did."

Bella doubted that. She found it hard to believe that her prim and proper aunt had a single rebellious bone in her body. But she remained quiet and allowed her to continue.

"This man was a stranger to me, just as Lord Belmont is a stranger to you. I met him once before our wedding and I found it outrageous that my father thought I could spend the rest of my life with a man I hardly knew. But as time went on, I began to embrace my situation. There was nothing I could do to change it, after all, so I had to make the best of what I had been given. Over time, my resentment turned to acceptance and then eventually happiness."

Bella made a face at that and Gertrude chuckled. "Yes, I am telling you that I grew to love him. An arranged marriage is not a death sentence, Bella. I know it must feel like one now but you can only trust that your father would not send you off with a man who will not take care of you."

"I hardly know if Father's intentions for me are pure," Bella couldn't help but say. "You were present this morning. I am nothing but an asset to be used when he deems fit."

"Your father loves you, Bella. He just does not know how to show it." Gertrude sighed, her hand reaching out to stroke Mr. Whiskers. "In any case, I want you to become more open to the idea of love in this marriage."

Bella couldn't imagine such a thing. How could she love someone she didn't know? How could she feel anything but resentment at being forced into a situation she wanted nothing to do with?

Before she could express that out loud, the butler knocked and entered, announcing a visitor. A few seconds later, Lady Eleanor breezed into the room with a bright smile on her face.

"Isabella!" Bella stood just in time to catch Eleanor's hearty embrace. "It's been so long since I have seen you!"

"Eleanor, I do not think it has been more than a few days," Bella told her with a smile tugging on her lips.

Eleanor pulled away, grasping both of Bella's hands in hers. "Yes, but it feels like—" She broke off, frowning as she took Bella in. "Have you been crying? Why have you been crying?"

"It's…a story for another time."

"And by another time you mean in the next few minutes." Eleanor slipped her arm through Bella's, holding her firmly to her side. She looked at Gertrude. "Good afternoon, Lady Wentworth. I hope you do not mind if I steal Bella away for a while?"

"By all means," Gertrude said with a soft smile. She'd always liked Eleanor. Everyone did.

Eleanor needed no more permission. She turned to the door and all but dragged Bella out of the drawing room.

"Now that we are alone," Eleanor began. "Tell me what has gotten you so upset."

"When we are truly alone," Bella assured her. She didn't want to talk about this so out in the open. She led Eleanor out to the gardens, her friend all but bouncing in anticipation.

The gardens made Bella feel safe. After Christopher's death, she would escape to the gardens whenever she needed time alone away from everything. To grieve by herself, to reminisce on the time spent with her wonderful brother. After a while, it became her place of happiness. After her debut, she rarely had the time to indulge in her solitude amongst the flowers any longer. Her focus had to be on securing her match.

Now that she didn't have to think about that any longer, Bella foresaw many more days spent alone among the rose bushes.

"What is it, Bella? Eleanor pressed as they delved down a stone-covered path. "I am positively overflowing with emotions, I declare!"

Bella laughed at that. Eleanor had been her friend for as long as she could remember. The day Bella had told Eleanor that Victor intended to send her to London for the Season, Eleanor had committed herself to convince her father to do the same. It hadn't taken much, though. Eleanor's father, the Marquess of Warmington, doted on Eleanor since she was her only daughter of four children.

She was an adorable beauty. Button nose, freckles splashed across both cheeks, pink lips that were always turned upwards. Eleanor and Christopher had always gotten along because they'd been very similar—vibrant souls that lit up the lives of everyone they were close to. Bella didn't know who she would be without Eleanor.

"I'm afraid my father has grown tired of my pickiness, Eleanor," Bella began with a heavy sigh. "I learned this morning that he intends to marry me off to the Viscount of Belmont. He is also the heir to the Earldom of Harenwood and the current earl happens to be a friend and business partner of my father. It was all very well thought out without my feelings considered, of course."

"Oh, Bella." Without warning, Bella was wrapped in another warm embrace. "I knew that something like this might happen but I'd hoped that you would be spared."

Despite her friend's morbid words, Bella laughed dryly. "I suppose I should have seen it coming as well. Father has never been one to be patient. And I have already debuted two years now. It was only a matter of time before he took the situation into his own hands."

"Have you met him?" Eleanor asked as she pulled away and they resumed their walk. "Your betrothed?"

"As luck would have it, I met him before our official introduction." Bella noticed Eleanor's look of confusion and went on, "I'd snuck out to visit the British Museum. I met him there and… well, let us just say that I did not make a very good impression."

"Verily, these vague responses shall surely be the end of me," Eleanor sighed. "Details, Bella! Details!"

"I accused him rather rudely of stalking me and eavesdropping on my conversation." Even though it had been a while since the encounter, Bella still couldn't help but wince at her poor manners. "I panicked when I saw him, you see. You know how many experiences I have had of gentlemen speaking against me to curry my father's favor so I couldn't be certain that he didn't have bad intentions. Now that I look back on it, I am ashamed of myself."

"Now this man is meant to be your husband." Eleanor sighed, shaking her head. "I would not have imagined such a twist of fate."

"Neither would I. Had you seen how shocked I was when I met him last night, you would have laughed right at me."

"Perhaps," Eleanor giggled.

Bella didn't have the strength to laugh this time. The more she spoke about her situation, the truer it became. A knot of frustration twisted within her. "What should I do, Eleanor? Father is adamant and I do not think he will change his mind. Aunt Gertrude wishes for me to accept my situation and embrace the idea that perhaps I may even grow to love this man, but how could I?"

"With time?" Eleanor caught Bella's shocked expression. "You've said it yourself, Bella. Your father does not intend to change his mind. You will be married to Lord Belmont whether you like it or not. If you continue to reject the inevitable, it may only lead to a joyless marriage. Perhaps you could try to make the best for your situation instead."

"I should just sit back and allow this to happen then?"

"You should look at the brighter side of things if this will happen," Eleanor explained gently. "Arranged marriages are common, Bella. Even though you may not wish to admit it, this was a possibility from the very start."

Eleanor was right. Bella didn't want to admit it. She didn't like the idea of this any more than the idea of marrying a man who so obviously wanted her father's wealth and title. But she also couldn't deny that there was merit in what Gertrude and Eleanor were saying.

"Tell me, Bella," Eleanor whispered excitedly in Bella's ear. "Is he handsome at least?"

Bella didn't even have to think about it. Those beautiful eyes had haunted her sleep and she had a feeling it would continue to do so for the days to come. She felt a genuine grin stretch across her face as she met Eleanor's excited eyes. "Infamously so."

***

Bella didn't see her father for the next two days. Things went back to near normalcy, to the point where she had nearly forgotten that her life was very close to being turned upside down. But then her aunt revealed that they had been invited by Lady Catherine to a luncheon and Bella felt that sense of dread all over again.

So much so that she could hardly keep it from showing. As she sat in the drawing room waiting for the carriage to be ready, her leg bounced, she picked at her nails, she nibbled on her bottom lip. More than once, Gertrude told her to calm down and stay still and she managed to do just that for only a few minutes. The worst thing was that Bella didn't know if she felt this way because of the expectations of her or who she was bound to see at the luncheon.

"I'm sure I do not have to tell you how to act during this luncheon, Isabella," her father said, cutting through her thoughts. He didn't turn to face her, standing by the window with his hands clasped behind his back. Ever the imposing figure that only struck deeper fear into Bella's heart.

Bella looked away from him. It only made her feel worse. "You do not. I know Father."

"Speak more," he ordered. "During the dinner, you hardly said a word. The earl even wondered if you were mute."

"I will."

"Lord Belmont will be present, as I'm sure you have already guessed. Make sure to make a good impression on him as well. I doubt you did a very good job during the dinner."

"Why?" Despite the dryness of her throat, the word was out before she could stop it. "The date is already set, is it not? What use will impressing him do?"

Victor turned to narrow his eyes at her and Bella immediately regretted her words. She looked back at her lap to avoid some of the wrath. "I hope you do not intend to have such a smart tongue when you are married. It is unbecoming of a lady."

"Yes, Father," Bella mumbled.

"The luncheon will primarily be used to discuss the details surrounding the wedding. I expect you to take part in the conversation as well. Lord Harenwood has informed me that Lady

Catherine is willing to assist Gertrude and you with the planning, since your mother will be absent."

Bella looked sharply at her father. No, surely he did not want the preparations to proceed without her mother's input? Would it have been so difficult to postpone it until Matilda and she could come to London? Bella burned with the urge to ask the question but she could feel her aunt's warning stare. She had to leave it alone, to attend to her father's wishes. Upsetting him may only do more damage.

Bella tried to quell her disappointment when the butler finally announced that the carriage was ready. She stood and followed her aunt out the drawing room like a woman making her way to the guillotine. Her ears rang, her eyes burning with tears that nearly escaped when she crawled into the carriage.

It took all her mental energy to hold them back and she was hardly aware of the silent trip, coming back to reality when the door opened and a footman held his hand out to assist her out of the carriage. He led them to the front door, Bella fighting her emotions all the way there.

But then the door opened and her eyes met the pair of icy-blues she had not been able to stop thinking about.

Lord Harenwood was not present, Bella noticed. Lady Catherine and Lady Amelia were. The two ladies, as well as Lord Belmont, stood facing Bella and her aunt in the foyer in greeting much like Bella had done a few days ago. But this time, her attention was solely on the gentleman before her, her feet taking her towards him without thought.

"Good afternoon, Lady Isabella," Lord Belmont greeted. As always, he looked at her as if she were an enigma he so badly wanted to figure out. Bella felt alive under his intense gaze.

"Good day, Lord Belmont." She remembered her manners a second later and sank into a curtsy. "Good day, Lady Catherine, Lady Amelia."

Lady Amelia curtsied as well, a broad grin on her face. But she was calmer than the last time Bella saw her, greeting Victor and Gertrude with grace. Lady Catherine on the other hand...

If countenances possessed a deadly power, Bella harboured a premonition that she would not have even surpassed the entrance. She couldn't decipher the look in Lady Catherine's eyes, but it was far from welcoming. The older woman managed to smother it a bit when she greeted Bella's aunt but Bella felt the lingering stain of it on her skin long after.

Pleasantries were exchanged quickly. Bella hardly paid it much attention, very much aware of Lord Belmont standing so close to her. She was right to describe him as infamously handsome. Bella didn't know how she'd manage to look at him directly before without blushing.

Before long, they were being led to the dining room where the luncheon would take part. Bella was very aware of the fact that Lord Belmont positioned himself next to her, even though she tried to fall to the back of the group.

"I take it you know now then?" he murmured to her.

Bella didn't dare to look up at him. "About our impending nuptials?" she asked, her voice deceptively calm. "So you were already aware, I see."

"I was," he admitted easily. "I did not think it my place to reveal the truth to you."

"As your future wife, I do not see why you would think such a thing. Is this what you want, Lord Belmont? To be married to me?"

"It matters not what I want."

That surprised her. Enough for her to break concentration and look at him. He didn't meet her eyes. "Then perhaps you and I are more similar than we thought. In any case, there is nothing I can do about the matter."

Bella left her tone hopeful, wanting him to catch on to what she was trying to say. She wanted *him* to do something about the matter. But Lord Belmont only shook his head. "Neither can I. I suppose we are stuck with each other, Lady Isabella."

"That is not what I wanted to hear," Bella admitted in disappointment.

"I'm beginning to learn that life rarely lets us hear the things we want."

The tone of sadness in his voice gave her pause but he was already walking away. Bella swallowed her questions and braced herself for what was to come. When Lady Catherine shot her another scathing look up entering the dining room, however, Bella wasn't sure just how well she would fare.

Chapter Eight

The tension in the dining room was enough to stifle England's strongest soldiers. Edward tried not to shift uncomfortably as the silence droned in his ears, the loudest he had ever heard. Lady Isabella didn't seem any more at ease with the unsettling quiet than he did. Though her face was the picture of impassiveness, Edward didn't miss the fact that she kept bouncing her leg beneath the table.

Stilted conversation began between Lady Wentworth and Catherine, though Catherine seemed unwilling to take part. Lady Wentworth's valiant attempts only stalled into another round of silence that Edward could not take anymore.

"Lady Isabella."

Lady Isabella jumped at the call of her name. Edward felt an odd urge to lean forward and shield her from his aunt's pointed stare.

"Yes, my lady?" Lady Isabella answered. Her voice was steady, to Edward's surprise. He knew very well how intimidating his aunt could be.

"Have you begun preparations for the wedding yet?"

"I have not. A date has not yet been set."

"That does not matter. There are many things that need to be done prior to setting the date. I thought you would have known that."

"Forgive me, my lady. It is my first time being married."

Edward bit his lip to keep from bursting out in laughter. He caught Amelia's mirth-filled eyes from across the table. She'd noticed Lady Isabella's slightly sarcastic tone as well.

"I thought you would have been more proactive, Lady Isabella. What a disappointment."

Lady Isabella wisely said nothing in response. Even so, she looked directly at Catherine and tilted her head to the side as if she was trying to determine if it was worth saying what was on her mind.

Before she could, Amelia cut in, "What do you think about roses, Lady Isabella? We could decorate the chapel with its vines and a few petals across the pulpit. We could even have your bouquet made with white and red roses. Of course, that would mean that the wedding would have to be a little later in the Season. Would you mind that?"

Lady Isabella blinked at Amelia. Edward couldn't but study the way she cocked her head in the other direction this time. "I do like roses," she admitted after a moment. "But my favourite flowers are lilies."

"As are mine!" Amelia exclaimed excitedly. "Then do you like the idea, only with lilies instead?"

"It does sound rather charming," Lady Isabella murmured, a small smile touching her lips.

"Doesn't it? And then perhaps we could even hand out flowers to each of the guests! Or would that be a little too much?"

"Pardon me, Amelia," Edward cut in. "But you have not asked me what I thought about the idea."

Amelia frowned at him, just barely stopping herself from rolling her eyes. "I'm sure you do not care about the specific details, Edward."

"On the contrary, I care very deeply. And just so you are aware, I prefer roses instead. They are far more romantic after all."

"That would be a solid sentiment had there been any romance involved in our union in the first place," Lady Isabella commented in a droll tone.

Edward shrugged, fighting the smile tugging at his lips. "Call me a poet then."

Lady Isabella mimicked Amelia's frown, giving him the same look she'd given his sister just moments before. Like she was trying to understand something.

"Enough," Catherine cut in sharply before she had the chance to reply. "The first thing that needs to be taken care of is the guest list. Then your dress, Lady Isabella. Have you purchased it yet?"

Lady Isabella shook her head slowly. "I have not."

"Goodness, there is clearly far too much that you do not know. Lady Wentworth, haven't you informed her of what is to be expected once she has secured her match?"

Lady Wentworth began her response but didn't get far when Lady Isabella spoke up again. "Allow me a bit more time, my lady, before such pressure is placed on me."

Her words sent the room into stony silence. Edward tensed, knowing what was about to happen. He didn't miss the way Amelia bit her lip in trepidation, a worried frown touching her brow.

Catherine's pinched face became even tighter, to his surprise. She seemed struck between shock and rage. "Pardon me?"

Lady Isabella opened her mouth and Edward was almost certain she meant to repeat herself. Edward didn't know if she was fearless or foolish. Or both.

"Pardon me," he spoke up, scraping his chair back as he stood to cover up anything that might be said, "but I am beginning to see that this conversation is best left to the ladies. I hope you will not mind if I go for a short walk?"

"By all means," Catherine responded dismissively. "We can handle this ourselves."

"Of that, I have no doubt." Edward pushed his chair in, then turned to Lady Isabella. "My lady, do you care to join me?"

Lady Isabella looked up at him with wide, emerald eyes. "Me?" she asked, incredulously.

"Yes, I was hoping to get to know you a bit more. I could take you on a tour of the manor." Edward looked over at Catherine. "Aunt, you will be able to handle the preparations in Lady Isabella's absence, I take it?"

Edward knew the moment his subtle taunt worked. His aunt raised her chin, disdain dripping from her gaze. She would have protested Lady Isabella leaving had he not insinuated that Catherine needed her.

"Go right ahead," she said. "I have a feeling Lady Wentworth and I will be taking care of most of the wedding preparations on our own anyhow."

Edward grinned. "Perfect. I shall call for a chaperone." He reached out a hand to Lady Isabella. She looked at it for a moment, lips thinning. For a moment, he thought she might turn him down.

But then she slid her hand into his. The moment their fingers touched, a shiver raced down his spine, his heart stilling in his chest. Edward curled his fingers over hers, lingering for a moment before he tucked her arm through his. The subtle scent of lavender washed over him and he nearly pulled her closer.

Edward could feel their eyes on them as they left the room. The moment the door closed behind them, Lady Isabella released a low breath.

"Do not breathe easy just yet, my lady," Edward warned. "I should fetch us a chaperone or my aunt will not allow us to be alone again."

She looked sharply at him at that but Edward tried not to meet her inquisitive stare, focusing instead on ringing for a maid. Within seconds, a young woman appeared, staying a few feet away, instantly falling into her role as a chaperone.

Edward turned and started down the hallway. He was still acutely aware of her arm still tucked into his. She was warm, soft.

"Thank you, my lord."

She spoke so softly that Edward almost didn't hear. "You're welcome, my lady. I could tell that the conversation was quickly growing uncomfortable for you."

"Uncomfortable?" She hummed in thought. "I would say frustrated instead. Overwhelmed, even. I did not expect to be faced with so many decisions at once."

"Forgive my aunt. She is known to be quite intense when she is interested in a task."

"Intense, you say..." Lady Isabella trailed off for a few seconds. Then she said, "I do not think she fancies me."

Edward chuckled under his breath, earning him an odd look from Lady Isabella. "You are not the first to think so. She just needs some time to warm up to you, that's all."

"If you say so."

She said nothing more. Edward found himself grappling with a way to continue the conversation and keep her talking. Questions rushed to his mind, ones he wasn't sure he should ask her just yet.

They continued walking, the sound of their steps swallowed by the carpet beneath their feet. He glanced down at her for what felt like the tenth time that day but her attention was on the paintings lining the walls. She studied them all with keen interest. When her gaze fell on a particular portrait hung above a mantle, she paused.

Edward followed her eyes. A familiar pair of blue eyes stared back at him, a smile forever frozen in time fixed on the young woman's lips. Contrary to her pleasant expression, everyone else in the portrait did not smile.

"That is my late mother," he said without thinking. "The Countess of Harenwood."

"I see." Lady Isabella's tone was gentle. She pulled away from him, approaching the painting. "She is beautiful."

"She is. This portrait hardly brings her justice."

Lady Isabella turned to look at him. Edward was stuck by the lack of pity in her eyes. He was used to pity, would always prepare himself for it whenever he mentioned his mother's death. But she stared at him with nothing but genuine curiosity as she asked, "How did she pass away?"

"A fever," he explained. "It took her quickly, before anything could be done about it. I did not get a chance to say goodbye. It is one of my biggest regrets, even though it happened when I was still a child."

He didn't know why he was telling her all of this. He rarely spoke about his mother except on those difficult days when he could not stop thinking about her. Even then, he only expressed his thoughts to Luke, only mentioning her lightly to Amelia, who hardly remembered her. Yet here he was, baring his deepest thoughts to a lady he hardly knew.

But she looked at him as if she understood him perfectly. "Regret will only eat at us, my lord," Lady Isabella said softly, turning her attention back to the portrait. "And yet it is but another way we keep the ones we love alive in our memories."

A lump formed in his throat. Edward remembered the day as if it had happened yesterday even though it had hardly already been fourteen years. He'd just turned ten-and-three, a few days before the argument that drove his mother out of the manor. He couldn't forget how upset he'd been at the thought of spending his birthday posing for a portrait he didn't want. Nor could he forget the small celebration his mother had with him in his chambers that same evening.

She'd always been so full of life, so kind and understanding. She was the strongest person Edward had ever known. The fact that she'd been taken by a fever felt like an injustice.

"You said us," he said after a long moment. "Have you been faced with the death of a loved one as well, my lady?"

"My brother," she answered. "It has been four years now and yet I am no closer to accepting his death than the day he left us. It was sudden as well. A carriage accident that killed him on impact."

"I'm sorry for your loss," Edward said gently because he didn't know what else to say. He was so used to receiving consolation that he hardly knew how to give it.

"I look for him in everything I do," Lady Isabella went on. Her eyes remained fixed on the portrait but Edward could tell she wasn't truly seeing it. "He is the reason I have grown so fond of history and literature. His favourite place to be was the British Museum and now, it has become my favourite as well. I do not get the chance to visit nearly as often, though."

"As did my mother," Edward expressed. "She was quite passionate about history and would take me to the British Museum often when I was younger."

"I wish I could have met her," Lady Isabella said with a soft smile. Edward didn't doubt that she meant it and that meant more to him than he could begin to say.

He turned to face her. "As two fellow lovers of history, perhaps we should make more of an effort to foster this relationship, my lady."

She mimicked him, turning to face him with her head tilted slightly. Edward was beginning to realize that she did that when she was confused or trying to understand something. It was surprisingly endearing. "What do you mean?" she asked.

"We will be married, my lady. Our opinions on the matter will not change that outcome. So, I propose that, rather than fighting it, we should embrace it instead."

Lady Isabella stared at him for a moment longer before a shadow of a smile touched his lips. "You say that as if you intended to oppose this union with the utmost conviction, my lord."

"Oh, come now, do not pretend as if the thought did not also cross your mind."

She shrugged but he didn't miss the shine of mirth in her eyes. "Then what do you propose then? That we do nothing about our situation?"

"That we make the best of our situation." Edward stuck a hand out. "A truce, my lady. That we at least attempt to be cordial with each other."

Lady Isabella looked down at his hand and, at that moment, Edward realized that he didn't just want to be cordial. He wanted more. He wanted to understand Lady Isabella, wanted to hear her laugh. Edward wanted them to be friends.

Then she smiled, a full-blown grin that lit her eyes and chased the shadows from his mind. Lady Isabella slid her hand into his, taking it firmly, and said, "A truce, my lord. You shall have it."

At that moment, he felt warring accomplishment and longing for something more.

Chapter Nine

Bella could not remember the last time she'd felt so relieved to see the inside of her chambers. Changing out of her gown was a tiresome process considering the fact that she wanted nothing more than to be alone. She spoke to Annie, telling her minor details about how the luncheon went, but Annie quickly understood that Bella was in no mood for conversation.

Bella hoped her maid would not blame her for it. After Edward and she had made their way to the drawing room—after the butler informed them that that was where the others had gone—Bella had been subjected to another long session of Lady Catherine dictating all the wedding details while making bold comments about how lacking Bella was. Bella had tried her best to remain polite, knowing that was what was expected of her. But all it did was leave her drained and tired even though the entire ordeal had lasted just a few hours.

Even Gertrude had seemed exhausted. As soon as they arrived home, she'd scooped Mr. Whiskers into her arms—who had come to greet her at the door as usual—and murmured that she was going to her chambers to take a nap. Bella wanted to do the same.

"Milady," Annie called now that they were finished with undressing. Bella had changed into a simple dress, decent enough to be worn to dinner later in the evening, she hoped.

"Yes?"

Annie reached into the pockets of her apron and pulled out a folded letter. "This arrived for you earlier this afternoon."

Bella accepted the letter, instantly recognizing her mother's perfect handwriting on the front. Suddenly, she didn't feel so tired anymore. "Thank you, Annie," she muttered, already opening the letter.

Annie curtsied and slipped quietly out of the room. Bella had already begun reading by the time the door clicked closed. She absently made her way to her bed, sinking on top as she hurried to read through the letter. The further she went, the more her heart sank.

It wasn't long. Her mother had always been a very direct woman, preferring to get straight to the point than waste her time with pleasantries. She began by stating that Matilda was not faring well. She was in a difficult state, with pain and fatigue throughout most of her days. Despite the nature of her news, the duchess maintained that Matilda was being cared for by several physicians and that there was no need for Bella to worry.

Easier said than done, Mother, Bella thought glumly.

The duchess also stated that she was aware of Bella's betrothal before the plans had come to fruition but had been sworn to secrecy. Even so, she wished that she could come to London to assist with the preparations.

Perhaps an hour ago, while enduring Lady Catherine's company, Bella would have longed for the same thing. But if her sister's state was as dire as her mother made it seem, Bella wouldn't want Matilda to make the trip. And there was no way she would let her mother leave Matilda alone. Her sister needed the duchess far more than Bella did right now.

Her tiredness forgotten, Bella got to her feet and hurried over to her table. She wrote a quick letter expressing her understanding of her sister's delicate condition and that there was no need for either one of them to overextend themselves. Gertrude was providing excellent care, after all.

She didn't mention her father's behavior nor Lady Catherine's unfriendliness. She simply expressed her worry for her sister, how much she missed them both, and left it there.

***

"No matter how many times I think about it, Bella, I can only come to one conclusion."

Bella watched as Eleanor dropped two cubes of sugar into her tea and stirred daintily. Her friend's eyes were alight with excitement, even though she was the picture of elegance. Bella turned her attention to the book in her lap. It was a history book she had been re-reading before Eleanor arrived. Now that she was here, Bella resigned herself to simply admiring the pictures.

"And what is that?" she asked, even though she could already guess what it was.

"He is smitten with you!" Eleanor abandoned her overly sweet tea and leaned closer to Bella. "Can't you see? He saved you from his bothersome aunt and then proposed that you two simply accept your situation with grace."

"Need I remind you that you did the latter as well?" Bella asked without looking up.

"I did but that is only because I know you and want the best for you. He does not know you and yet he seems *so* willing to be in your company."

Bella couldn't help but laugh at that. Eleanor was a hopeless romantic, down to the blood in her veins. "I think he was just a little eager to escape the room as much as I was. Nothing more to it, El."

"You are not willing to see what is so clear before you," Eleanor said with a disappointed shake of her head. She reached for her tea again and took a sip, even though Bella was certain it had long since gone cold. "But when you finally become aware of the truth, do not say I did not warn you."

"Is it a warning?" Bella asked her with a crook of her brow. "Or encouragement?"

Eleanor grinned. "Whichever you prefer, my wonderful friend."

Bella just shook her head, laughing softly. The moment Eleanor arrived, she'd demanded to know every detail about what happened the afternoon before. Bella was beginning to wonder if she might have said a little too much.

Smitten? Nonsense. She hardly knew the viscount and he hardly knew her. No one could become smitten with someone in such a short span of time, could they?

Bella thought of that lopsided grin he'd given her after their shaken hands on their truce and her heart skipped a beat. It had skipped a beat then as well, but she assumed it was due to his uncanny handsomeness. No sane lady could look at a face like that and be completely normal, could they?

Her reasoning did not sit as well as she'd hoped.

Someone knocked on the door. A second later, the butler stepped in to announce that they had two visitors.

"The viscount?" Eleanor whispered excitedly to Bella.

Bella didn't answer, looking back at the door with her heart still in her chest. The next moment, it sank to the pit of her stomach when Lady Catherine walked in, followed by Lady Amelia.

Isabella rose purely on instinct, though every bone in her body wanted to ask the older woman to leave. "My lady," she greeted with a curtsy. "I did not expect you to visit this afternoon."

"Save the gratitude," Lady Catherine said dismissively. She sauntered over to the largest armchair in the room and sat. "We have much to discuss."

Isabella quelled her annoyance, turning her attention to Eleanor instead, who had risen with her. "This is my friend, Lady Eleanor. Eleanor, please meet Lady Catherine and Lady Amelia."

"A pleasure," Lady Amelia said. She looked as lovely as ever, her cheeks flushed as she sank into a deep curtsy. When she straightened, her eyes fell on the tight ringlets in Eleanor's hair and she gasped. "Oh, I love your hair, my lady! You look beautiful!"

"Why, thank you." Eleanor beamed, touching the ends of the curls. "It took quite some time this morning. Mother nearly had to drag me out of my chambers because it didn't seem to be coming to an end. But it was all worth it."

"Yes, I agree." Lady Amelia was standing in front of Eleanor in a second. They grasped hands as if they'd been friends for years. "Do you know how to do it yourself?"

"As a matter of fact, I do." Eleanor led Lady Amelia over to the couch in the middle of the room, across from where Lady Catherine sat. "Would you like me to show you how to do it yourself?"

"I would love that!"

Bella watched the exchange with slight amusement. She supposed she shouldn't be surprised that Eleanor and Lady Amelia got along so quickly. They were mirrors of each other, feeding off of each other's excitable energy.

Lady Catherine, however, clearly didn't appreciate the line of conversation. She had a fan in her hand and she snapped it into the palm of the other, cutting into their conversation. "Enough of the silly chit-chat," she hissed. "We didn't come here to waste time, Amelia. Now Lady Isabella," Bella stiffened when Lady Catherine's piercing gaze turned to her, "where is your aunt? She needs to be here—"

"My ladies!" Gertrude entered the room in a flourish, her skirt pinched in her hands. It came as no surprise to Bella that Mr. Whiskers was right on her heels. "I did not know that you would be coming today."

"We didn't think it made sense to send word," Lady Catherine said dismissively. Gertrude's smile tightened at that. She was the epitome of proper and the proper thing to do—according to Gertrude—was to send a calling card if one planned to visit someone's residence.

She didn't say that, however. She bustled over to Bella's side and steered her towards the chaise lounge so that they were all sitting facing each other.

"I must say," Gertrude went on. "I truly admire your dedication, Lady Catherine. Your assistance with the preparations is truly appreciated."

Lady Catherine raised her chin. "You're lucky that I am here at all. Now, let us go on with it, shall we? We shall be hosting a ball to celebrate your engagement. The theme of the ball is yet to be determined, if there will be a theme at all, but I am considering a dress code—"

"Wait, pardon me," Bella cut in without thinking. She frowned at Lady Catherine. "Engagement ball? I do not recall hearing anything about a ball."

Lady Catherine looked at her as if she was trying to reign in her annoyance. "That is why I am informing you of it now. I came to the conclusion last night. Of course, it shall be held at our residence—"

"My lady," Bella cut in again. She knew she was making a mistake by doing so twice but she didn't care. Her head was spinning. "But why do we need an engagement ball?"

"Surely you are not asking me that question?" Lady Catherine released a breath of frustration. "How else did you intend to announce your betrothal, Lady Isabella? Did you think the banns would be enough? Goodness, what would you do without me?"

Bella curled her hands into fists, hiding them in her lap. She leaned back and tried to quell her irritation.

"As I was saying," Lady Catherine went on, "I was considering a dress code, though I am not sure what yet."

"How about red and white?" Eleanor suggested. "If you intend to use the idea of the red and white roses, it would be rather fitting, don't you think?"

"A foolish suggestion," Lady Catherine dismissed. Eleanor deflated and Bella felt another surge of anger.

"I like that idea," Bella stated. "I have a number of white gowns that will be perfect for the occasion."

"That matters not. You may simply purchase a new gown if you need to." Lady Catherine paused, pursing her lips in thought. "Natural colors," she decided. "Brown, green, cream."

"Cream is hardly natural, Aunt Catherine," Lady Amelia commented.

"Natural colors," Lady Catherine said again. She nodded to herself. "Good. Now that we've gotten that out of the way, there is the matter of the guest list. Lady Wentworth, I hope you will not remain silent this entire time."

Bella was more than happy to hold her tongue. After yesterday, she'd learned that there was no use making suggestions when Lady Catherine would only dismiss the idea or ignore it altogether. It didn't make it any less frustrating to see, however. Especially when it was aimed at Gertrude or Eleanor. Lady Amelia seemed to know how best to handle her aunt, using a blend of compliments, acquiescence, and a little force to get her own ideas considered.

This was her wedding. An engagement ball that would be thrown in her honor. Even though Bella was no happier about this arranged marriage today than she was yesterday, it bothered her that her thoughts on this entire matter were constantly being pushed to the side. Whether it be her father or Lady Catherine, Bella met it everywhere she turned.

She tried not to sigh, resigning to waiting until Lady Catherine grew tired and left. Her gaze fell idly on Mr. Whiskers. The cat flicked his tail every time Lady Catherine spoke. Bella entertained herself by guessing when the cat would get annoyed enough to get up and leave altogether.

She counted to forty seconds before Mr. Whiskers stood, hissed, and curled his entire body at Lady Catherine as if she were a threat. Bella held back her giggle as Gertrude hurried to put her cat out before Lady Catherine could get very upset by it. Bella silently lamented the act. The cat was her only entertainment and it gave her a bit of pleasure knowing that even Mr. Whiskers could tell that Lady Catherine was quite unpleasant.

But now that the cat was gone, and the conversation no closer to ending, Bella's mind wandered to the dark-haired gentleman that had been occupying her thoughts as of late.

And she couldn't help but wonder if he fared any better right now than she.

***

Edward wanted to drive his head through a wall.

The sensation did not happen often, even when he was in his father's presence. For the most part, he could focus on actual business matters rather than the tense relationship between them. But today, Edward found that he could not focus on the meeting he was currently in. His thoughts were trained solely on the vivacious blond lady he would soon call his wife.

"Have I told you that you will be attending Lady Portia's soiree tomorrow evening?"

Edward looked at his father with a frown. "You did not. Don't you think it's a little too late to inform me of this?"

"Better late than not at all," Humphrey stated with a dismissive wave of his hand. "I have already stated that you will be in attendance."

"And you?"

"Perhaps not. I have not yet decided."

Small mercies. "Lady Portia...is she the wife of the Marquess of Jonesons?"

Humphrey nodded, twisting his quill pen between two fingers. "Her husband, though with his age puts him halfway in his grave, has always been a close friend of our family so one of our attendances is mandatory. Your betrothed will be attending as well. It will be your first event as a betrothed couple, so an impression must be made."

Edward scoffed a laugh. He should have known there was some advantage to this. Fostering an old relationship hardly seemed like reason enough to take part in this event. Edward considered his response for a second and settled on leaving the matter be. He could do nothing about it, after all. And, since his truce with Lady Isabella, he saw no purpose in protesting.

"Very well," he stated.

Humphrey regarded him quietly for a moment. Then he said, "I must commend your change of attitude towards this, Edward. I had been expecting much more of a fight. You have always been a lot like your mother in that regard."

Edward let the mention of his mother slide over his skin where it didn't bother him. At least, he tried.

"I'm sure you are well aware of how beneficial this union will be for our family. And you will have to take a wife sooner or later. What better time when the duke's daughter remains untethered?"

"Perhaps," Edward stated noncommittally in the hopes that his father would just move on.

"His Grace has many business connections. Our monopoly of the tea industry will be far quicker and easier with his help."

"Shall we continue then?" Edward gestured to the ledgers they had both been compiling.

Humphrey stared at him a moment longer and Edward was almost certain that he would lash out at him. But then he simply nodded and they resumed their task in silence. Edward was so grateful for the break that he didn't even question his father's unusual behavior.

He gave himself fully to what he was doing but Lady Isabella lingered on the fringes of his mind. It took him a few more seconds to peel back the layers of his usual annoyance towards his father to find the tremor of excitement hidden underneath. He would be seeing Lady Isabella again. Perhaps attending might not be so bad after all.

Chapter Ten

"Milady?" Annie touched Bella gently on the shoulder. "Milady, are you all right? Do you feel unwell?"

The worry in Annie's voice was what brought Bella from her reverie. She blinked, looking at her maid with a tender smile. "Annie, you are a gifted genius."

Annie's eyes widened, her cheeks flushing shyly. "Thank you, milady, but I do not know what you mean."

Bella turned back to the tall mirror next to her armoire and shook her head in disbelief. How couldn't she understand what she meant? It was right before her eyes! Her deft, gifted fingers had heated half of Bella's hair into loose curls, pining most of it to the top of her head. Tendrils framed Bella's face and the nape of her neck and a small headpiece was nestled within the heavy updo. Her cheeks had been dusted with the lightest touch of rouge to accentuate their already rosy pallor, and just a bit brushed over her lips. Annie had chosen a lovely green gown Bella had not worn in some time, pairing it with matching gloves and Bella's favorite fan.

She looked absolutely lovely.

"Father will be pleased, won't he?" Bella asked, twirling in the mirror. "Surely he will have nothing bad to say about my appearance?"

"He would not, milady." Annie beamed at Bella. "I must say, milady, your excitement for this ball is rather surprising."

"Isn't it? I can hardly understand it myself."

It wasn't entirely the truth, Bella knew. When her father had informed her that she would be attending—indirectly through the butler, of course—she'd felt dismayed. With everything happening, she was in no mood to attend any event of the Season. But then the butler had also informed her that Lord Belmont would be arriving to escort her and she found her spirits instantly lifted. Bella didn't bother to question why.

"I should go, Annie," Bella said, fetching her fan before hurrying to the door. "Father will be upset if I keep him waiting."

"Only His Grace?" Annie asked softly. Bella only laughed but didn't answer.

Her heart raced as she made her way down to the drawing room. Bella couldn't recall the last time she'd been this excited to attend a soiree. Perhaps when she first debuted. But she found it hard to believe that her heart had skipped so many beats at that time, or that she had raced down the steps of the grand staircase with such fervor.

Bella drew to a halt as she arrived to the door of the drawing room, realizing that her father might be waiting for her on the other end. She brushed her hands over the skirt of her dress and flicked a few of her curls away from her face. She looked absolutely darling, she knew, but she wouldn't dare give her father any reason to criticize her.

To her relief, only Gertrude occupied the room. Even Mr. Whiskers was absent.

"Bella," her aunt called as she entered, setting her book aside. "Good. You're here. I was hoping to speak with you before you left."

"Won't you be attending the soiree as well?" Bella asked with a frown. Her aunt was dressed rather elegantly and she doubted she'd gotten so put together just to go to bed.

"Victor and I will be attending in a separate carriage," Gertrude answered. "I have reason to believe that Lord Belmont will be here at any moment to escort you separately."

Separately? Bella thinned her lips, putting a hand to her chest. Her heart seemed to have stopped beating for some reason.

"In any case," Gertrude went on, oblivious to Bella's dilemma. "It is about your wedding. I know Lady Catherine had gotten a little...overzealous the last time she was here. I hope you do not feel too overwhelmed."

"Overwhelmed would be an understatement, Aunt Gertrude," Bella answered honestly.

Gertrude shook her head disapprovingly. "I prepared you for this, did I not? It is expected that a lady will make the necessary preparations for her wedding. You only get one, after all. It wouldn't do for you to leave it in the hands of another."

"I would not say that I am leaving it so much as it is being taken forcefully. Lady Catherine would not listen to anything I wished to say."

"It is your wedding, Bella," her aunt pressed. "You should take control of the discussion since you will be the one most affected by it. She left you a list of things you need to take care of, didn't she?"

Bella nodded, resisting the urge to roll her eyes at the memory. Lady Catherine had asked for paper and ink and had tasked Bella with writing down everything she needed to do in preparations for the engagement ball and the wedding. Bella had left the list on the mantle above the hearth in her chambers and desperately hoped that a gust of wind would blow it into the fire underneath.

"Do not ignore it," Gertrude warned. "Accept the help, but do not let her control you."

Bella contemplated the warning for a moment. No one had been able to get Lady Catherine to listen, not even Gertrude. Would she listen to her?

Do I even care?

Bella nodded but got no chance to respond when the butler arrived, informing them that Lord Belmont had arrived and waited for them in the foyer. Gertrude pulled herself to a stand and linked arms with Bella to escort her to see him in place of her father. Bella was secretly grateful for the company. With the way her heart began to race the closer she got to the foyer, she wasn't entirely confident that she would not say or do something stupid.

Lord Belmont did not see her right away. He leaned against the threshold by the door, arms crossed, gaze fixed on the door. It gave Bella the opportunity to take him in, to admire him however unwittingly. She had no choice to. He was the picture of gentlemanly elegance. His black boots shone like the floors he stood on, his hair styled away from his face. The cut of his waistcoat and tailcoat accentuated his tall, lean build. As she drew closer, Bella found herself wishing he would look up so she could see his eyes.

And when they did, they were darker than she'd ever seen them. She wondered if it had anything to do with the lighting in the foyer or perhaps the way he took her in. Slowly, from the top of her head to the point of her toes. Bella was grateful for the tinge of rouge on her cheeks that hopefully hid her blush at his bold gaze.

"My lord," she greeted, her aunt releasing her as she sank into a curtsy.

Lord Belmont didn't answer. He only stared at her, his gaze fixed solely on her face. Silence stretched on for a few more seconds until Gertrude said, "My lord?"

He blinked, looking at her as if he hadn't realized that she was standing there. "Oh, uh, good evening, my ladies. I..." He trailed off again when he caught Bella's eyes.

She couldn't look away from him. She could sense her aunt's gaze upon her, yet Bella was rendered speechless, immobilised by his intense stare.

"His Grace and I shall follow in a carriage shortly after you," Gertrude spoke again. Lord Belmont blinked and looked back at her. Bella remembered to breathe. "By all means, my lord."

Lord Belmont straightened and then offered his arm. Bella didn't hesitate to take it. She looked back at Gertrude to say her goodbyes but fell quiet when she saw the twinkle of...something in her aunt's eyes. Humor? Intrigue?

Bella didn't get the chance to figure it out because Lord Belmont was already steering her out the door. The fresh evening air cooled her hot cheeks. As they made their way to the carriage, Bella was suddenly grateful for the gloves she wore. She had a feeling her hands would be a clammy mess otherwise.

"Forgive me if I made you uncomfortable, my lady," he spoke after a few moments of silence. "I was speechless by your beauty. I wished to tell you how lovely you looked but couldn't find the right words."

Bella nearly tripped over her own feet at those words. "I think you've articulated it quite well, my lord," she managed to say.

"Have I?" He paused. "A well-read lady like yourself deserves a far more eloquent compliment."

"A compliment is a compliment, my lord. No matter how it is said. And I thank you. You look rather dashing this evening."

"It is only proper since I will be attending with a beautiful lady on my arm."

Oh, heavens. Bella hadn't imagined that the viscount would have such a smooth tongue.

She was saved from having to respond when they made it to the carriage. He helped her in and she was given a few seconds to collect herself while he jogged around to the other side before climbing in as well. They took off in silence.

"Tell me, Lady Isabella," Lord Belmont spoke after a few minutes. "Are you dreading attending this soiree as much as I am?"

Bella's lips twitched. "Not at all, my lord. I have not attended a ball in quite some time. I am looking forward to dancing until my feet fall off."

"Dancing?" Bella glanced at him just in time to see the look of horror he gave her. "I cannot imagine anything worse."

"You do not enjoy dancing, my lord?"

"I do what I must for the occasion. Perhaps with the right partner, I could dance all night as well."

"Surely you are not considering that we dance every set together?"

"That depends, my lady. Are you the right partner?"

Bella laughed without thought. Lord Belmont's deep chuckle rumbled next to her. "Well, we shall see about that, shan't we? But I jest about dancing all night. As someone who spends most of her time in the library reading, I have very little stamina to keep up with such a thing."

"Oh, a woman after my own heart," Lord Belmont said, clutching his chest in an exaggerated manner that made Bella laugh once more. "First the British Museum and now this. Next, you're going to tell me that your favourite exhibit happens to be in the Egyptian Hall."

Bella grinned broadly. "Brace yourself, my lord."

Lord Belmont matched her grin with equal fervor. "We must pay it a visit then. It would be a shame if we didn't."

"I would love that," she answered and was surprised by how much she meant it. Not for a second did she think that she would have felt such kinship with the man she was being forced to marry.

Lord Belmont nodded happily but said nothing more. They drifted off into comfortable silence that only lasted for a few minutes. As it happened, Joneson Manor was not very far from where Bella lived. The soiree was already well underway but they were not the only ones arriving. It took a few more minutes for their carriage to make it to the front of the manor. A footman opened the door and helped them out. Bella felt a little more comfortable when she took Lord Belmont's arm once more.

Together, they followed the rest of the arriving guests into the manor to the ballroom. Bella felt at ease. Happy, almost.

That feeling vanished into horror when they entered the ballroom and all eyes fell on her.

Chapter Eleven

It felt as if the room went still. Edward knew that that couldn't be the case, that it must just be a figment of his imagination. But from the way Lady Isabella stiffened next to him, he wondered if she thought the same thing.

But then, just as quickly, it seemed as if everything went back to normal. A hum of chatter hung over the small orchestra in the corner of the ballroom. The refreshments table was heavily populated and nearly every person in attendance had a drink in their hands. As they made their way into the depths of the soiree, Edward could feel eyes following them as they walked. Whispers trailed in their wake.

He supposed he should have known better than to assume that others would not have something to say about their betrothal. The ton had something to say about everything. They were no different.

"I see my friend, my lord," Lady Isabella said. Edward felt a sudden rush of cold as she pulled away from him. "I shall go to greet her."

"My family is already in attendance," Edward said. He spotted Amelia standing uncomfortably next to Catherine but his father was nowhere to be found. He still wasn't certain if he had attended.

"You should go to them," Lady Isabella urged. "I shall greet them soon"

She didn't give him much time to answer before she turned and quickly made her way to the other side of the room. Edward couldn't help but watch her as she approached a brown-haired lady who greeted her with a bright smile. Edward resisted the urge to follow, turning to his sister and aunt instead.

Amelia's face lit up when he approached. She rushed to his side. "Edward, thank heavens," she breathed.

"Why do you sound relieved?" Edward asked with a laugh.

Amelia shot a glance behind her at Catherine and leaned in to whisper, "Aunt Catherine is making me stand with her because she does not see any of her friends in attendance."

That didn't surprise him. Catherine didn't have many friends but she was far too proud to be caught standing alone. Edward patted his sister's shoulder in a comforting manner. Amelia, who could find companionship even with the unlikeliest creatures, must have been enduring immense distress throughout this time.

Edward drew closer to his aunt but before he had the chance to say anything, she frowned at him and asked, "Did Lady Isabella and you arrive on your own?"

"We did."

She scoffed. "In my time, a lady would never be seen in private with her intended spouse. Lady Wentworth should have been with her. Or her father. What were you two thinking?"

"That it is not back in your day," Edward answered with ease. He had no intention of making his aunt ruin his night. He ran his eyes through the crowd of people and they came to rest on Lady Isabella once more. Her friend and she had melted back to the wall, talking earnestly to each other.

"Where is His Grace then?" his aunt went on, undeterred. "Will he not be in attendance?"

"Lady Wentworth and he have just arrived, Aunt Catherine," Amelia answered. She sounded tired, as if she had been enduring this for too long and didn't know how much longer she would last.

"Where?" Catherine sounded incredulous but Edward saw the moment she spotted them. "Oh. Well, they should have arrived with the two of you. Now the entire ballroom is talking about your betrothal and you."

Edward couldn't help but sigh. "I thought you would have liked that, Aunt Catherine."

"Not when it invites scandal! I—"

"Aunt Catherine, tell me who has gotten you so upset, and allow me to go and set them straight."

Edward tensed at the familiar voice, not looking at the lanky gentleman as he approached. He didn't have to look at him to know that he was exactly the same as when Edward last saw him.

Unruly sandy hair, an ever-present smirk on his lips, and a snuffbox tucked into his waistcoat. The smell of brandy and tobacco tended to follow him everywhere.

"Edward, it has been a while, hasn't it?"

Resigned, Edward turned to face him. Lord Thomas Granville cocked his head to the side and grinned as if he knew something that Edward didn't. Edward struggled to keep the disdain off his face.

Thomas was Catherine's nephew from her late husband's side of the family. Catherine and he had always been close, which meant that Edward saw him far more often than he'd liked to.

"It is good to see you, Thomas," Edward said politely and tried not to cringe at the fact that he'd just lied through his teeth. Thomas' eyes sparkled as if he heard the deceit too.

"You as well, cousin," Thomas chirped, making Edward grind his teeth. Thomas was moving on to Amelia though. "You as well, Amelia. My, it feels as if every time I see you, you are even more beautiful than the last."

Amelia did not like Thomas either. Unlike Edward, she was far better at hiding it. She smiled politely. "I think the last time we saw you was three years ago, Thomas. Have you been on your Grand Tour?"

"Something like that," Thomas said noncommittally. "Boring details, I assure you. But I thought to attend this evening's soiree since it has been some time since I have seen my lovely aunt."

"I appreciate the sentiment, Thomas, but I am in no mood to entertain you," Catherine said moodily.

"Worry not. I do not need to be entertained when I can simply seek it myself." At that time, the orchestra changed their song and couples began making their way to the center of the ballroom. "And right on time too. Do you think I have enough time to find a dance partner, Edward?"

"I'm sure you intend to try," Edward drawled and Thomas chuckled.

"You know me too well." Thomas sauntered off at that, much to Edward's relief. He tensed a few seconds later when he noticed that he was heading in Lady Isabella's direction.

"Edward, let's dance!" Amelia suggested excitedly to him. Edward nodded absently even as he felt an odd sensation come over him watching Thomas bow to the ladies. He waited for the lady next to Lady Isabella to take his hand. From the way she smiled, Edward could almost believe that he was asking her to dance.

But then Lady Isabella glanced at her friend, then at Thomas, before putting her hand in his. Edward had somehow made it into the center of the room with Amelia in his arms, watching them approach.

Lady Isabella smiled at something Thomas said. Then laughed. Edward heard a buzzing in his ears. He tried to look away but couldn't. He matched steps with Amelia, hardly hearing her as she chatted away to him. It was an upbeat song and so the dance did not require anyone to be in close quarters with their partner.

Yet when Lady Isabella laid her hand on Thomas' shoulder and laughed when he twirled her around, Edward gritted his teeth. When Thomas took the chance to whisper something to her at a slow part of the song, he felt his body grow hot.

Only when Lady Isabella's eyes darted to the side and met his did he finally look away.

Chapter Twelve

Bella wasn't entirely certain about Lord Granville. He was kind enough, charming at first. When he first approached she'd mostly ignored him since it seemed as if his attention was focused mainly on Eleanor. But then he had asked *her* to dance and Bella, seeing no reason why she would say no, accepted his invitation.

Now she was beginning to regret it. The first thing she noticed was that Lord Granville talked *a lot*. He never seemed to run out of things to say, his lips moving constantly as he went from one topic to the other. Bella managed to keep up for a while but quickly realized that Lord Granville did not need a response to anything he said. Bella was a wall and he liked speaking to it.

At first, she didn't mind. Bella played along, laughing in the appropriate moments as they danced their first set. Soon enough, Bella just went along with the movements of the dance—and then her eyes fell on Lord Belmont.

He was dancing with Lady Amelia and their eyes met for a moment but Lord Belmont quickly looked away. Bella frowned. There was something very dismissive about that small moment.

"Goodness, is it over already?" Lord Granville complained once the set came to an end. Bella still had her eyes on Lord Belmont, watching as he escorted Lady Amelia back to where their aunt stood. "What would you like to do, my lady? Or shall we wait for the next set?"

"The next set?" Alarmed, Bella looked sharply at Lord Granville. She took in his cheek grin and let out an uneasy laugh. "Surely you jest?"

"That all depends on what you think about the idea, my lady," Lord Granville purred. It made her shiver in disgust. She took a discreet step back.

"I do not think it would be proper for us to do such a thing, my lord."

"Ah." His shoulders sagged in obvious disappointment. "Then it is a jest, my lady. Shall we?"

Without much warning, he grasped her hand and slipped it through his arm. Bella was left with no choice but to follow him. She sent another look over her shoulder, but she couldn't find Lord Belmont with all the people suddenly in her way.

Gertrude was now standing by Eleanor, discreetly eyeing Lord Granville as he approached.

"Good evening," he said as he deposited Bella to Gertrude's side. "I'm afraid we did not meet before. Had I known you were available, my lady, I would have jumped at the chance to ask you to dance the first set."

Bella blinked, glancing at her aunt. Lord Granville's words hung heavily in the air as he swept into a deep bow. Gertrude's face didn't move. She didn't even attempt her usual polite smile.

"What a lovely thing to say to a group of ladies, Lord…"

"Granville," he supplied. He straightened and scratched the back of his head in a sheepish manner that didn't do anything to lessen the uncomfortable air he'd just created. "Forgive me, my lady. I find that I tend to misspeak when I am faced with such beautiful ladies."

"Hm," was all Gertrude said, which Bella understood meant that she was not impressed by this man's attempts.

"Have you been in London for long, my lord?" Eleanor spoke up. Clearly, she was uncomfortable with the tension and was quickly hoping to overcome it.

"This is where I was born and raised, my lady," Lord Granville answered. He began patting his chest as if looking for something. Bella felt her aunt aghast when he withdrew a snuff box. Lord Granville caught Gertrude's underlying horror and sighed before putting it back away. To Eleanor, he continued, "But I have been away for some time, you see. I came back because it has been some time since I have enjoyed the London Season and I wanted to see where the days will take me."

"Then are you looking to settle down?" Bella couldn't help but ask. She wasn't entirely surprised when Lord Granville shook his head.

"I only wish to spend time with family and enjoy myself."

"Are there any of your family members in attendance?" Gertrude asked as she snapped her fan open and waved it at her face.

"As a matter of fact, they are." Lord Granville turned and grinned at something. "Though my dear cousin, Lord Belmont, likes to pretend that we are not related."

"That is because we are not." Bella's heart fell to the bottom of her stomach when Lord Belmont appeared suddenly. He stood next to her, putting one shoulder before her as if he was trying to shield her from Lord Granville.

Lord Granville grinned broadly, patting Lord Belmont on the upper arm. "He is a prickly one, you see," he said to Eleanor, who watched the exchange as if a scandal was enfolding before her eyes. Bella couldn't blame her. Anyone with eyes could see that Lord Belmont was not fond of Lord Granville. She wasn't entirely certain if Lord Granville was oblivious or was simply playing the fool.

"I came over to see if you were bothering Lady Isabella and her family," Lord Belmont said. He hadn't looked at her once, his narrowed gaze focused entirely on the lanky man before him.

"Bothering is a strong word," Lord Granville drawled and, to Bella's complete surprise, her aunt scoffed silently under her breath. "I was simply making conversation. Isn't that what one usually does at events such as these?"

"Only if one is welcomed. Do you know the host, Thomas?"

Bella couldn't help the surprise she felt at Lord Belmont's tone. She hadn't heard him speak so coldly before. But then again, she remembered, she hadn't known him for very long.

Lord Granville's smile remained fixed on his face but Bella didn't miss the glint that appeared in his eyes. Silence followed Lord Belmont's words and for a moment, Bella thought that an argument was about to ensue.

Obviously sensing it as well, Gertrude came to the rescue. "Lord Granville, I do not think you have expounded on your familiarity with Lord Belmont. Did you say that you two are cousins?"

The cheer returned to Lord Granville's demeanor as if nothing had happened. "We most certainly are—"

"By marriage," Lord Belmont said through gritted teeth. "He is Aunt Catherine's nephew from her late husband's side of the family."

"Which would make us cousins," Lord Granville said simply. He reached into his waistcoat once more for his snuffbox as if he was tired of waiting. "I must say, it was very interesting meeting you all. I shall leave you to enjoy the rest of the soiree."

With that, he sauntered off. Bella watched him go then shifted her gaze to Lord Belmont. She could all but feel the frustration roiling off him in waves.

"My lord—"

He turned abruptly to face them. "Please, enjoy the rest of your evening."

And then he was gone once more, leaving an uneasy ache in the center of Bella's chest.

Chapter Thirteen

Bella thought she was losing her mind.

She hated it, hated how quickly she'd gotten attached to the idea of a friendship with the viscount that she was already fearing it was gone. Everywhere the lord went, Bella's eyes followed. She begged him silently to look at her, to give her a glimmer of hope that there wasn't a rift already forming in the fragile partnership they had created. But he ignored her the entire time.

Bella was tired of herself at this point.

Nearly the entire soiree went by in that manner. She passed from gentleman to gentleman, dancing nearly every set despite what she'd said earlier about her lack of stamina. Bella didn't know if it was because of her aunt's insistence or the fact that Lord Belmont was doing the exact same thing but she barely got much time to rest. Whatever breaks she found was used to catch her breath and find Lord Belmont if he had gotten lost in the crowd of people.

She just couldn't shake the feeling that something might be wrong. He was ignoring her, that she was certain of. But why? What had she said? Or done? Or did it have something to do with Lord Granville and nothing to do with her? Not knowing was driving her insane, even though it shouldn't. They hadn't known each other long enough for this to bother her and yet here she was.

"Goodness, thank heavens." Eleanor grasped Bella's hand tiredly and sagged against the wall. Bella's lips quirked in amusement.

Her poor friend had been just as active as she'd been. At first, Eleanor had been excited. She'd stated to Bella the moment she saw her that she was eager to dance the night away. But now that the ball was coming to an end, there was faint sheen of sweat on her face and a flush on her cheeks.

"You are a genius, Bella," Eleanor panted. "Did you find this corner to hide from the gentlemen? They are relentless!"

"They are only relentless because they are smitten with you," Bella said with a smile.

Eleanor tucked herself behind one of the potted plants nearby. "You are kind but that is a lie. Everyone seems to be in high spirits, that's all. Speaking of high spirits," Eleanor gave her a curious look, "why are you hiding in the corner."

"For the very same reason."

"Truly? I thought Lord Belmont and you would have been dancing this set."

"I thought so as well," Bella couldn't help but say. She watched him with a blond hair lady as they moved slowly together for the waltz. Watching him in such an intimate dance made her chest ache.

"Does it have anything to do with her?" Eleanor didn't have to point, didn't have to say a name, for Bella to know who she was talking about. Just as she had been watching Lord Belmont all night, Bella knew that Lady Catherine had been watching her.

Even now the older lady stood in the very same spot she had been all night. Now and again, she would be preoccupied with someone else. But for the most part, Lady Catherine glared at her as if she was waiting for Bella to make a mistake.

"Do not let her bother you, Bella," Eleanor spoke again, sensing Bella's discomfort. "She seems to have nothing better to do than to watch you all evening. That is hardly your problem."

"I know," Bella said, but that was easier said than done. Between Lady Catherine's constant judgment and Lord Belmont's silence, Bella didn't know what to do with herself.

The song trailed to an end and Bella resisted the urge to look back at the viscount. She didn't want him to catch her staring at him.

"Bella," Eleanor whispered excitedly. "Lord Belmont is approaching."

"Is he?" Bella feigned nonchalance even as she looked up to confirm her friend's observation, her heart hammering painfully against her ribcage. She watched as he cut a path through the crowd, guests stepping out of his way on instinct. The pair of electric blue eyes focused solely on her sent shivers skittering over her skin. This is what she'd gotten used to, she realized. Not being ignored, but him staring at her as if she was the only thing that existed.

"My lady." Politely, Lord Belmont swept into a low bow, then offered his hand. "I'd hoped to ask you for the honour of sharing this next dance."

Bella swallowed and prayed that her face did not betray the state of her heart. "The soiree has nearly come to an end, my lord," she told him.

"That is so. I wanted to save the last dance for you." He smiled at her.

Eleanor gasped at Bella's side, clutching her arm. Bella felt heat race up the back of her neck and she struggled to maintain her composure.

"How romantic," Eleanor sighed.

Bella silently agreed. For now, she didn't have any words. She wordlessly put her hand in his and let him lead her to the center of the room. Bella was struggling to remember how to breathe when he pulled her into a light embrace as the orchestra began a slow sonata.

"Have you enjoyed your evening, my lady?" Lord Belmont asked.

"I...have. Though I'm sure I could have found better ways to spend my evening."

"Hush now, my lady," he said with a chuckle. "Lest our fathers hear us."

"Is yours in attendance? I have not seen him all evening."

"He is, somewhere around here. Apparently he does not care much for these events to actually take part in it."

Bella imagined the earl sitting at a crowded table with other lords playing cards while the smell of scotch and tobacco hung in the air. "If he is enjoying himself then I suppose there is no harm in his thinking. I cannot say the same, however. I long to return home."

"Right as you've begun your dance with me? I am hurt, Lady Isabella."

Bella looked sharply at him, not entirely sure if the mirth she heard in his voice was just a figment of her imagination. "It has nothing to do with you, my lord. Perhaps if we had spent more time together, I would have enjoyed the evening a little more."

It might have been her imagination but it felt like his hands tensed against hers. She focused on the room moving over his shoulder, though it was barely more than a blur. She hardly thought of the steps to the waltz, their movements so synchronized with each other that it felt as if they had danced together a million times before.

"Forgive me, Lady Isabella." He spoke so softly that she wasn't sure if she'd heard him right.

"For what, my lord?" she asked, leaning back slightly to look at his face.

He didn't meet her eyes, his jaw ticking. He seemed…uncomfortable. "I have neglected you all evening and for that I am sorry. I hope it has not put you under unnecessary scrutiny."

"Worry not, Lord Belmont. I do not think others truly care about what we do. Other than Lady Catherine, perhaps."

"Does that mean you accept my apology?"

Bella made a show of thinking about it before she said, "Before I answer that question, answer mine. Was it all simply to ask for the last dance?"

Lord Belmont shook his head. "I do not think so."

"You do not think so?" she echoed, incredulous.

His discomfort deepened and Bella instantly regretted how persistently inquisitive she could be. Despite that pinch of guilt, she didn't take back her words, secretly hoping that he would answer her.

"I noticed when Lord Granville danced with you," he said at last.

Bella only stared at him, uncertain of how to proceed with that information. "And…you do not like him," Bella tried to conclude.

"I do not. Is it obvious?"

"Very much so, my lord," she said with a laugh. She didn't truly understand. How could his dislike for one person affect how he treated another? But Bella was so relieved to know that it had nothing to do with her that she didn't bother to question him further on the matter.

"I ask again then, my lady," he continued, his voice a little lighter. "Do you accept my apology?"

"I do but you should know that I am not a very forgiving person."

Lord Belmont chuckled. The sound washed her with heat and brought a smile to her lips. "Allow me to make it up to you then, my lady."

The set came to an end and they were forced to step away from each other. Bella didn't move even as everyone else began to return to their previous places and neither did he. They stayed in the center of the room simply smiling at each other.

"Wait for my call, my lady," he said. "It shall be a surprise."

"Do not let me wait long then," she said in return.

"I shan't." He offered his arm and she eagerly took it. Bella felt a rush of relief when he lead her over to Gertrude instead of where Lady Catherine stood. They listened together as the host made her final speech of farewell before everyone began filing out of the ballroom. Her cheeks ached from her smiling as they made their way to their carriage, alone once again, and they spoke about their love of history all the way to her residence. Even as he escorted her inside, Bella felt as if she was floating on air.

She didn't question what any of it meant. She didn't want to think about it. The only thing she did was make her way to her bedchamber, changed, climbed into bed, and hoped Lord Belmont's smile would follow her into her dreams.

Chapter Fourteen

The next morning seemed brighter than usual. Bella stared out the window of the drawing room, wondering how the sun could possibly shine so brightly or how the birds could sing so beautifully or how the wind could feel so gentle on her cheeks. She sighed happily, sipping her hot chocolate.

"Did you hear what I just said, Isabella?"

Her father's gruff question was not enough to break her fully from her daze. Bella set her cup down and hummed, "Yes, Father."

He grunted as if he did not believe her but it was the truth. Gertrude and he had been discussing last night's soiree and the impact the news of Bella's engagement might have had. Bella didn't care to take part in the discussion.

But it was clear that her father did not intend to let her off easily because he asked, "What do you think about what we've just said?"

Bella tried not to sigh, knowing that her aunt would not appreciate the unladylike action and her father's borderline pleasant mood could quickly vanish if she did. "I do think we made an impression," she answered. "While others were talking about our betrothal, I did not hear any negative remarks."

"Neither did I," Gertrude expressed. "There was even a mention of you in the scandal sheets. Did you see?"

Bella shook her head, not caring to lie. Gertrude's shoulders sagged with disappointment. Mr. Whiskers, sitting by her feet, flicked his tail as if he too didn't like that response.

"You really should stay up to date with the news of the ton, Bella," her aunt chastised. "But yes, Lord Belmont's and your engagement was mentioned rather favorable."

"That isn't something to praise, Gertrude," her father said as he gorged on his breakfast of meat and bread. "Gossip will always invite negativity. You should make sure to learn that as well, Isabella."

"Are you not pleased by it, Father?" Bella asked him, picking back up her cup.

Victor shrugged. "I am not displeased but such things should be taken lightly. You know very well how fickle the ton can be. If we place too much attention on the things they say then we will suffer when their tongues turn against us."

"Oh come now, Victor," Gertrude said amiably. "I think such a thing is a good sign. We can take advantage of it when planning Bella's engagement ball."

Bella cringed inwardly at the mention of the ball. She'd almost forgotten about it. The usual dread the memory of it would drag up did not come this time, however. She supposed a ball with Lord Belmont wouldn't be so bad...

"Have you begun the preparations?" Victor asked Gertrude. Bella turned her attention back to the window and hoped that they wouldn't try to involve her in the discussion.

"It is underway," her aunt answered. "Lady Catherine has been quite helpful in managing the smaller details so, for that, we are grateful."

"And you, Isabella? Have you assisted?"

"Yes, Father," Bella answered easily. She'd expected it even though she hoped that she wouldn't have to. "Lady Catherine has left me a list of items to take care of."

"Good. You should listen to her. She may be cold but she is wise about such things."

"As is Aunt Gertrude," Bella couldn't help but say. "I do appreciate her help but I am certain Aunt Gertrude and I could handle it ourselves."

"Bella, hush now," Gertrude said quickly, though not as sharply as Bella expected. "We should be grateful for any assistance we receive. Planning a wedding is no small matter, after all. It grows even more difficult when an engagement ball is added into the mix."

Bella bit her tongue and looked out the window. She was in too good of a mood to continue an argument she had no hope of winning.

Victor said nothing, his attention now on the morning's copy of *Times.* Silence filled the room, which Bella didn't mind. It didn't even bother her when he got up a few minutes later and walked out of the room without a word.

Her mind was on the days to come, on the call that a certain gentleman said he would send.

***

It wasn't often that Edward could sit peacefully during breakfast and listen to nothing but silence. He sipped his coffee, his mind drifting to Lady Isabella despite the fact that he had been trying to read the morning newspaper since he sat down. He swore he could see her smile in the twist of the letters, could hear her laughter when he turned a page.

The silence did not last long however. Not when both Amelia and Catherine sat before him.

"Wasn't it fun, Edward?" Amelia asked. "Last night's soiree, I mean. There was so much dancing! I met so many new people and I have already sent letters to four of my new friends."

"I am not surprised to hear that," Edward said honestly. "It sounds like you enjoyed yourself."

"I did! But then again, I usually enjoy myself at such things. Especially when I am not being forced to stand in one place."

Amelia boldly shot her aunt a glance, who matched it with heated fervor. To Edward's surprise, Catherine didn't bother to comment on that.

"But I want to know about you, Edward," Amelia went on. "How did you enjoy yourself?"

"It was not as bad as I thought it would be," Edward confessed. He gave up on the newspaper and focused entirely on his coffee.

"Surely that has something to do with Lady Isabella," Amelia said with a cheeky grin. "Did you hear what others were saying when they saw you dancing the last set together?"

Edward didn't care about the ton's opinion. He found it entirely tiresome and draining to indulge in such things. But...

"What were they saying?" he found himself asking before he could stop himself.

"I overheard two ladies saying that they thought you two looked quite good together. A lovely couple, is what they said. And they were looking forward to seeing your union. The other things I overheard were very similar."

Edward fought his smile by finishing his cup of coffee. He wasn't a fan of the hot beverage but he needed it after arriving home so early this morning. He didn't have the luxury of sleeping in like Amelia did but he had always been an early riser.

"You should not pay such things any heed," Catherine snapped, dousing Edward's pleasure with her negative tone.

Amelia frowned in confusion. "Why not? I thought you would be pleased."

"I would be pleased if that was the only thing others were saying. Apparently, there is already a rumour being spread about Lady Isabella." Catherine narrowed her eyes at Edward, gripping his arm tightly. "Others are saying that she had flirted with another gentleman."

"Lady Isabella would not do such a thing," Amelia said instantly, shaking her head.

"Oh?" Catherine crooked a brow at her. "And how would you know? You have not known her for long. You cannot possibly know if she was truly a coquette—"

"Enough, Aunt Catherine," Edward snapped. He pulled his arm from her grasp. "As you say, it is just a rumour. And if we should pay little heed to what Amelia has overheard then we should do the same for what you have as well."

Catherine clearly didn't like that. Her lips pinched together in disapproval. "Nasty rumours always have some truth to it, Edward. I am not saying that it actually happened. I am only saying that you should pay keener attention to Lady Isabella going forward, lest she brings you down with her if she ends up in a scandal."

"Like Amelia, I choose to believe that Lady Isabella would not do such a thing. Not only is she a proper lady but she has a good enough head on her shoulders to know how detrimental such an act would be to her reputation. She wouldn't dare."

"I agree," Amelia chimed in with a decisive nod.

Catherine sat stiffly. "It is only a warning, Edward. Because I am concerned for you."

Edward softened. Deep down, he knew his aunt only wanted the best for him. She'd always been a prickly person and everything she'd gone through in life had only made her even more so. Despite the way she spoke and acted, he didn't doubt that she cared about Amelia and him.

That was the only reason he relaxed and nodded. "I understand, Aunt Catherine. I shall keep that in mind then."

"That is all I ask." And then she went back to her silence. Even as Amelia went on to another topic that forced Edward to take part rather than daydream about a certain blond-haired lady, Catherine said nothing. It was odd for her to be this quiet.

Something about it made Edward contemplate what she'd said just a little deeper than he'd expected to.

Chapter Fifteen

"What do you think about him?"

Bella looked in the direction Eleanor indicated and had to stifle the laughter that raced up her throat. They were close enough to the gentleman in question that he would certainly hear her if she did.

"Eleanor, you did that on purpose," Bella accused. She turned to the pond of quacking ducks and focused her attention on feeding them. She tried to ignore her giggling friend by her side but failed horribly.

Hyde Park was usually well-populated during this time of day. Eleanor had arrived earlier this afternoon asking Bella to accompany her for a walk through the park with their maids in tow. Since Bella had spent most of her morning trying to read and finding that she could do nothing but think about Lord Belmont, she'd jumped at the chance.

They'd only been at the park for almost an hour and Eleanor had already made her forget all about the viscount. They were currently assessing the liberation many gentlemen were taking with their fashion, though Bella felt a little badly about it.

"It is quite tight, don't you think?" Eleanor asked her before descending into another fit of giggles that nearly brought her to her knees. She gripped Bella's arm to keep her upright but Bella was of little help herself. She could hardly hold back her laughter, tears springing to her eyes.

The gentleman glanced at them curiously, clearly overhearing their laughter. Bella wondered if his attire was on purpose. If he had meant to squeeze himself into such tight breeches that the seams were ripping and the buttons of his waistcoat were straining against his rotund stomach.

"Over here," Bella said between giggles and steered Eleanor over to a nearby bench. "We need to regain ourselves. This is quite unbecoming of us."

"Not to mention a little unkind." Eleanor wiped her tears and visibly forced herself to sober up. Bella didn't miss the fact that she was trying her best not to look back in the gentleman's direction. "Now I feel a little bad. I hope he did not realise that we were laughing at him."

"He seems to carry himself with enough confidence that he would not even consider the possibility." To be safe, Bella fixed her attention on the ducks swimming atop the pond nearby. "If Gertrude were here she would scold us silly."

"Only if she did not laugh herself," Eleanor said with a sigh. "Ah, that was truly needed. I was feeling a little down this morning but this walk has certainly lifted my spirits."

"Down?" The unsightly gentleman forgotten, Bella twisted to face her friend. "Why?"

"It isn't anything concerning," Eleanor assured. "I was only thinking about last night and well…since you are my closest friend, I feel I can be honest with you."

"Of course, you can," Bella expressed earnestly. She tried not to show her instant worry at Eleanor's words. For as long as she'd known her, Eleanor rarely showed negative emotions. At one point, Bella thought Eleanor was immune to things like anger and sadness.

Even now, Eleanor smiled despite the faint sheen of distress in her eyes. "I was thinking about how romantic it was for Lord Belmont to save the last dance for you and well…I cannot wait until I can experience that."

"Eleanor…"

"Oh, don't look at me like that," Eleanor said with a laugh. "I am not sad about it. I am…impatient. I am just eager to find a gentleman who I can court seriously."

"Ah, I see." Bella relaxed, a smile stretching across her face. She'd been worried for a second there. "That seems like an easy thing to fix, El. You know as well as I that you have a score of men hoping to have your hand in marriage."

"But will they give me *romance?* That is what I want."

"Forgive me but I fail to see how Lord Belmont's words last night could have inspired all of this."

"Oh, you wouldn't understand. You have never really cared about romance the way I have. Had you truly looked at the way Lord Belmont looked at you, as if he hung on your every word, then perhaps you would understand where I am coming from."

"Well, I do not. Lord Belmont and I have agreed to be friends but that is it. I doubt he has any intention of truly courting me."

Eleanor began to respond but then a broad grin stretched across her face instead. Her eyes fell on something over Bella's shoulders. "Why don't I ask him myself then?"

Bella frowned, then turned to look behind her. Her heart sprang into her throat when she spotted Lord Belmont atop a black beast of a horse. And he was coming towards her.

It was quite unfair, she thought, how perfect he looked every time she saw him. As if he had molded every inch of his body before leaving, as if the wind and the elements bowed to his will and ensure that there was nary a hair out of place. Bella rose as he grew nearer. Eleanor was saying something to her but she didn't hear a word of it. All of her attention went to trying to calm her rapidly beating heart.

He brought the stallion to a slow stop and dismounted easily. He didn't bother to tether the beast. Lord Belmont only patted his neck and said something to him and the stallion snorted gently in response. It seemed he was good with all sort of animals, not just cats.

"My ladies," he greeted with a small smile. "What a surprise to see you both here."

"Yes, what a lovely surprise," Eleanor agreed happily. "And what a lovely coincidence, my lord. There is something Bella and I have been meaning to—"

"Eleanor, I'm sure Lord Belmont is too busy for such things," Bella chimed in quickly. "There's no need to bother him."

"It is never a bother, my lady," Lord Belmont said politely. Bella's chest caved while Eleanor clapped happily.

"Ah, such gentlemanly behaviour is always nice to see, my lord," she said. She paused, giving a mischievous look. "But I shall save it for another time."

Bella breathed a discreet sigh of relief. She didn't know if Eleanor would have really asked the question but she was happy to be saved from finding out.

Lord Belmont looked a little confused at that but the expression cleared quickly from his face. "I am happy to see you, Lady Isabella I have just received an invitation to Lady Wentworth's literary evening. I am looking forward to it."

"I hope it is to your liking, my lord," Bella responded. "My aunt hosts these evenings quite often so she has become quite entertaining at it. And you will quickly learn that she is quite well-read also."

"I do not doubt it. Will you be in attendance as well, Lady Eleanor?" he asked.

"Yes, I shall be. Though I'm afraid I am not a lover of literature as Isabella and you are." She sighed. "I hope I will not fall asleep."

"I won't allow it," Lord Belmont stated. "I'm sure we could find something you would be entertained by. Won't we, Lady Isabella?"

"It is a foolish hope, my lord," Bella sighed. "I have been trying for some time now and I have long since given up. She is a lost cause."

"Yes, I'm afraid there is no helping me. But I do intend to support Lady Wentworth as much as I can."

"That only shows your character, Lady Eleanor," Lord Belmont said, which had Eleanor beaming.

"It is always lovely running into you, Lord Belmont," she said. "You are always so full of compliments."

"I can hardly help myself when faced with such lovely ladies like yourselves."

Eleanor slid her arm through Bella's and squeezed. Bella knew exactly what that meant but ignored it.

"Were you going for a ride, my lord?" she asked him.

"I was. It is a hobby of mine and I find that the fresh air Hyde Park provides has always put me in a better mood. I did not, however, expect there to be so many people here."

"It is quite busy, isn't it?" Bella agreed. "El and I thought to isolate ourselves by feeding the ducks. Then we would have gone for a walk through the flower garden."

"I hope you will not mind some company?" Lord Belmont asked.

Bella's heart skipped a beat but she managed to maintain her composure. "What about your horse, Lord Belmont?"

"He is trained well enough to follow along. You needn't worry about him."

That was all Bella needed to hear. She finally released the smile she had been holding back. "By all means, my lord."

Lord Belmont returned her smile and, for a moment, it felt as if they were the only two people in the world, the only two that mattered. Then Eleanor tugged on her arm and she came back to reality.

"Wait, one moment." Lord Belmont looked around for a moment and then held up a finger before jogging away. Bella watched as he approached a flower peddler and began reaching into this waistcoat.

"He is buying you flowers, Bella!" Eleanor whispered excitedly in her ear. "And you tell me you do not think he is trying to romance you?"

"Perhaps that is not the case," Bella mumbled but she was transfixed, watching as Lord Belmont exchanged a few coins for two bouquets of peonies.

"Goodness, you are blind as a mole," Eleanor sighed but she left it at that when Lord Belmont began jogging back up to them.

"I hope these are to your liking," he said with an uncharacteristically shy grin. Then he handed one to Bella and the other to Eleanor.

"My, you are the sweetest gentleman in all of London, Lord Belmont," Eleanor sighed, smelling her flowers.

Lord Belmont grinned but Bella knew he was waiting on her response. He watched her intently, every move she made examined carefully. She tried not to look up at him until she sniffed the flowers once more and the smiled. Truthfully, she didn't care about how they smelled. The pink petals were in full bloom and they were perfect with a few droplets of dew still on them. Fresh, beautiful flowers would make any lady happy.

But receiving it from Lord Belmont...

Bella didn't know what to do with the odd sensation in her chest when she met his eyes. "I love them, my lord."

And the relief and pleasure that visibly washed over him did something to her she simply could not explain.

Chapter Sixteen

The evening could not come quickly enough. Parting ways with Lady Isabella earlier in the afternoon had only whet his appetite for her company even further. He returned home late afternoon, went straight to his study, and tried to focus on work rather than the fact that he would be seeing her for the literary evening soon.

When it was time for him to get ready, Edward agonized over the minute details regarding his attire, something he'd never cared to do before. Edward had always done what was expected of him when it concerned social situations and his wardrobe was no different. He need only keep up with the slow pace changes of modern fashion and that would be enough.

This time, however, he weighed the idea of wearing a lily attached to the lapel of his tailcoat, remembering that they were Lady Isabella's favorite flower. Or perhaps bringing his green ornate pocket watch because he thought he might have heard her mention that that was her favorite color. Even when he was finally dressed, he dismissed his valet and paced his room wondering if he should follow his mind and bring another bouquet of flowers for her since she'd so clearly enjoyed the one she'd received that afternoon.

A knock on the door of his chambers pulled him from his obsessive thoughts. "Come," Edward called gruffly.

To his surprise, Amelia was the one who slipped into the room. Edward paused to look at her with a frown. "Amelia, what are you doing here?"

"I was on my way to the duke's residence when it occurred to me that we could arrive together," she explained. She mimicked his frown. "What were you doing?"

"Nothing," Edward answered dismissively. But the moment he ran his fingers through his hair and Amelia narrowed her eyes at him, he knew that wouldn't be enough to kill her curiosity.

"Hm." Amelia wandered closer, tapping an index finger on her chin in thought. "This doesn't seem like nothing. You seem quite on edge. Are you nervous about seeing Lady Isabella again?"

Edward quickly turned away, stalking to his table in the hopes that his sister hadn't seen his shock at how easily she'd seen through him. He supposed he shouldn't be surprised though. Amelia was much like their late mother in ways she would never get to experience herself, with the same perceptive nature that made it difficult for anyone to hide anything from them. Edward, especially.

"You are nervous!" she concluded with a gasp. "My, Edward I had my suspicions, but I did not think you would prove me right so easily."

"Prove you right regarding what?" he asked as he busied himself with the assortment of watches he had locked in a box. He knew how odd he seemed doing such idle work, understood very well that he probably was not helping his case by doing this.

"You are smitten with Lady Isabella," Amelia stated smugly. "Do not bother to deny it either. You are not very good at hiding the way you feel."

"Nonsense, Amelia." Giving up on the busy work, Edward attempted to escape altogether. He grabbed his coat and made for the door. Amelia fell right on his heels.

"Why is it nonsense?" she asked. "It is completely reasonable in my opinion. Lady Isabella and you share a lot in common, not to mention the fact that she is beautiful and smart. I'm sure there were many other gentlemen who found themselves in your shoes, though none of them could ever call her their betrothed."

Oh, Edward didn't doubt it either. He'd seen how many gentlemen had all but crawled over each other to dance with her during Lady Portia's soiree. Lady Isabella had accepted them all with that lovely, gracious smile of hers. Every time he thought of it—of how Thomas had held her that evening—brought on a wave of dark emotions Edward did not want to focus on.

"She does not wish to marry me," Edward pointed out as they made their way to the ground floor. "If it were up to her, I'm sure she would not even entertain this union. And I feel the same. However, since we have decided to make the best of our situation, we have become friends. Nothing more."

"Yet," Amelia sang happily.

Edward rolled his eyes. If he entertained this any longer, he was bound to say something he didn't want to. "Where is Aunt Catherine?" he asked. "I thought she would have traveled with you."

"She did. She is in the carriage."

Edward paused at the door. He turned to his sister with raised brows. "So she has been waiting for us this entire time?"

Amelia began to nod and then stopped, her brows also shooting upwards. "She will be furious," she breathed in a horrified tone.

Edward chuckled and opened the front door, admitting a gust of uncharacteristically chilly wind despite the fact that summer was approaching. "Serves you right for meddling in matters that do not concern you."

"She will be mad at you as well," Amelia pointed out.

"Perhaps, but your scolding may be worth it."

Amelia pouted adorably and Edward resisted the urge to pull her playfully into his arms. He didn't think she would appreciate the damage it might do to her perfectly coiffed hair.

They were halfway to the carriage when she spoke again. "You say Lady Isabella wants nothing but a friendship, Edward. But what do you want?"

Edward took a moment to respond. Perhaps it had something to do with the somber way she'd voiced the question but he didn't even consider ignoring her. Instead, he said, "I want the same" and tried not to be bothered by how much that felt like a lie.

***

It was always a treat watching Lady Isabella when she did not know that she was being watched. Edward knew that he did not have much time to do so. As their carriage pulled closer to the residence, it was only a matter of time before she realized that she was being observed. So he savored the brief seconds as if they were water and he had been quenched for days.

She stood outside her gate speaking to a young lad, a soft smile on her face. A gentle wind tousled her hair, which she had opted to leave most of out. The rest was pinned to the top of her head in intricate curls that must have taken considerable skill and time.

The dress she wore was befitting the evening ahead of them, a pale blue dress that accentuated her rosy cheeks and the light in her eyes. Edward swallowed thickly, watching the way she interacted with the boy in front of her. She did not look up when the carriage approached. She nodded along to whatever it was he was saying as if he was the only thing that required her attention.

Edward wondered if she did that on purpose. Having been on the receiving end of such rapt attention before, he knew just how special it made one feel.

At last, as the carriage pulled to a stop, Lady Isabella handed the boy a letter, patted him companionably on his shoulder, and watched as he sped off. She stared at him for a few seconds before she finally turned to the carriage.

"Goodness, this lady will be the death of me," Catherine muttered in disgust. "What in heaven's name is she doing out here at this time? It is almost dark! And she stands there so boldly as if she has no reason to be ashamed."

"Why should she?" Amelia asked before Edward got the chance to rush to Lady Isabella's defense. "It is her home, is it not? Why wouldn't she be allowed to move about as she wishes?"

Catherine sneered at that. "She is expecting guests. There is a proper way of going about these things."

"Her aunt is the one expecting guests," Amelia maintained. Her tone was light but Edward was sure she was getting a little irritated by Catherine's constant criticism of Lady Isabella just as much as he was.

Catherine tensed, clearly intending to continue but Edward was in no mood to listen to any more of her bickering. The carriage had already stopped and Lady Isabella was now tilting her head in expectation.

He exited first, then remembered his manners a second later. He resisted the eagerness mounting in him as he helped his sister and his aunt out of the carriage as well.

Lady Isabella smiled a little when he approached. "My lord and ladies," she greeted as she sank into a curtsy. "Welcome. My aunt and I appreciate your attendance."

"Where is your aunt then?" Catherine asked, looking down her nose at Lady Isabella. "If you are out here to greet us then she might as well be too."

Lady Isabella straightened and faced Catherine directly. She didn't bother to smile as she said, "My aunt is waiting for your arrival inside. You are not the first guests to arrive so she has been quite busy entertaining those who are here."

Catherine clearly didn't like Lady Isabella's bold nature. They were like two lions facing each other, one trying to assert her dominance and the other unmoving in the face of it. For now, it was only a standoff but Edward had a feeling that a true fight would break out eventually.

"It sounds as if we are missing the evening then," Edward chimed in before his aunt could respond. "Shall we go inside?"

Lady Isabella looked back at him and her eyes lit up. "Allow me, my lord."

With that, Lady Isabella turned and made her way up to the front door as they followed behind her. A slightly frazzled looking butler met them on the other end and Edward had a feeling he had spent some time looking for Lady Isabella. He greeted them and took over the task of escorting them to the drawing room where everyone else was.

Lady Isabella did not look back as she walked, which left Edward staring after her. It felt as if he was always doing that lately. Staring when she wasn't looking, observing the minute details that surrounded her, watching the way she interacted with the world around her. The more he watched, the closer he was drawn into her orbit.

He wanted to speak with her a little longer but the chance for that disappeared when they entered the drawing room. True to what she had said, the room was already full with a number of familiar faces and Lady Wentworth was in the middle of what seemed like a riveting story. Even so, she paused to greet them warmly, stood to usher them to their seats, and returned to hers to continue.

Edward didn't listen to a single word. Lady Isabella sat across from him, in his direct line of sight. Easily seen but unable to be interacted with. Much like the exhibits at the British Museum he enjoyed so much.

This might be a long evening.

Chapter Seventeen

Bella's prayers had been answered. Nearly an hour into the evening, Lady Catherine complained loudly about a megrim and left. Bella nearly sang in relief. Now that the lady was not present, the room instantly felt lighter. It was as if everyone had been holding their breaths, tense, with her here and could finally relax the moment she was gone.

Though Bella couldn't relax completely with Lord Belmont sitting directly across from her. She tried to maintain propriety, remembering her aunt's warning earlier this afternoon, so she didn't dare to look at him too often. If the wrong person in the room noticed, there was no telling what kind of rumors would go around. But it seemed Lord Belmont did not care about that possibility. He had been staring at her from the moment they sat down.

She couldn't deny that she liked the attention. She was used to it, having been courted before, but it was always done under a layer of English propriety. Lord Belmont's action were open, honest. Bella wondered if she would be able to see right through him if she dared to meet his eyes.

The evening progressed with each guest sharing their favorite readings from whichever book they had brought with them. Before long her aunt turned to her, indicating that it was her turn.

Bella discreetly cleared her throat and picked up one of Jane Austen's work, Sense and Sensibility. She couldn't help glancing up at Lord Belmont before she began. He sat with his legs crossed, a finger touching his chin in quiet observation. Bella's heart began to race.

"I was inspired by Marianne Dashwood's character," she began in a clear tone and then began to read. She held the attention of the entire room, her voice rising and falling as she read through a long passage she felt best described the character she mentioned. When she was finished, she explained why it resonated so much with her and then fell quiet, letting the discussion she had just inspire spread throughout the drawing room like a wildfire.

Unable to help herself, Bella looked at Lord Belmont again. He grinned at her and mouthed, Fine choice.

Her answering grin touched her lips without thought. She only bowed her head slightly in gratitude. Suddenly, she wished her aunt had allowed her to sit with him but Gertrude had adamant that they should maintain a proper distance, lest there be rumors.

Soon enough, it was Lord Belmont's turn to read. He chose a passage of Shakespeare. Bella had never been fond of Shakespear but listening to Lord Belmont recite his work made her appreciate it far more. It had much to do with the cadence of Lord Belmont's voice, the deep baritone rumbling through the room capturing everyone. It was also in the way he gestured with his hand as he became immersed in the passage he was reading. When he was finished, he even inspired a small round of applause.

Bella could not take her eyes off him. She didn't know what it was, why he was making her heart race like this.

The evening continued as expected but Bella could not focus on anything else. At long last, her aunt announced that the discussion was over and everyone was free to engage in light conversation and refreshments. Bella sprang to her feet and instantly made her way over to Lord Belmont.

He came to a slow stand as she approached, brows raised expectantly. Bella opened her mouth…and then realized a second later that she hadn't a clue what she wanted to say.

Mirth filled his ice-blue eyes. "Would you like a glass of lemonade, my lady?" he asked.

Bella closed her mouth and nodded as her cheeks warmed in embarrassment. He grinned as if he knew what she was thinking and led her to the small table laden with lemonade, cakes, and sandwiches for her aunt's guests. He poured her a glass and then another for himself. Then they drifted over to the corner near the hearth, away from everyone else.

Bella sipped her lemonade, watching the room in the silence. Lady Amelia was still sitting with a glass of lemonade in her hand, talking excitedly with Gertrude and a gentleman Bella did not know. Everyone else seemed to have found a conversation partner. Snippets of conversation floated over to their quiet corner, much centered around more discussion of literature and upcoming events of the season.

"I must say, Lady Isabella," Lord Belmont spoke, breaking the quiet. "The reading of the passage you chose was quite riveting. I have never read any of Jane Austen's work but now I know I must."

"You have not?" she echoed in surprise. "That is quite...unexpected. She's grown quite fashionable as of late."

"Yes, I'm afraid I am behind on the times. I have never been one to keep up with the latest trends, I'm afraid."

Bella laughed. "Worry not, my lord. If a book is the only reason one would be deemed unfashionable then many would suffer. Or perhaps many would do as you wish and read more."

Lord Belmont returned her laughter and it warmed Bella from the inside, chasing away the dregs of that unusual nervousness she had been suffering from as of late. "That reminds me, my lady. I thought Lady Eleanor would be in attendance this evening?"

"She came down with a slight megrim," Bella explained. "Though I'm sure she was quite happy that she had an excuse not to come."

"Yes, I'm sure she was relieved," Lord Belmont chuckled. "Perhaps as relieved as you looked when my aunt left earlier."

Bella looked at him in surprise. "Did I look relieved?"

"Quite so. It looked as if you even murmured a prayer of thanks."

His tone was full of humor. Even so, Bella felt as if she had to tread lightly with the sudden change of topic. Lady Catherine was his aunt, after all. Even though she was certain Lord Belmont knew how Lady Catherine could be, Bella didn't think it proper to complain about his aunt's behavior directly to him.

"If she is suffering then I do think it is in her best interest to return home so that she can rest," she said after a moment.

"A nice, diplomatic answer," he mused. "Worry not. I shan't reveal your secret."

Bella sipped her lemonade to hide her smile. "I have a confession to make," she said. Catching his eye, she laughed. "And it has nothing to do with anyone else but me."

"I am all ears, my lady."

"I do not like Shakespeare in the slightest." She said it simply but Lord Belmont looked at her, even took a step back, as if she had just revealed that she was with child.

"How could you not?" he asked, incredulous.

"I find his writing tiresome and overbearing. I have never enjoyed his work, from his plays to his sonnets and anything in between. It is a vice, I suppose, since he is so loved by upper society that it is almost a crime not to enjoy his work."

Lord Belmont shook his head, still in obvious disbelief. "That is certainly true. But I suppose it should not surprise me that you are not like anyone else."

Momentarily distracted, Bella asked, "Why should it not surprise you?"

"This is coming from the same lady who snuck out of her home to visit the British Museum of all places—"

"Hush!" Bella whispered frantically even though no one was close enough to overhear them.

Lord Belmont chuckled. "My point is, you have proven yourself quite different from the average London lady so your revelation will only add to it."

"Well, you may have to take back your words, my lord. My confession was that, despite the fact that I have never enjoyed Shakespeare's work, I find myself riveted by your reading. So much so that I have a new appreciation for his work."

Lord's Belmont's grin was full and cheeky. She had no choice but to match it.

"So you mean to say that I have converted you, Lady Isabella," he teased.

Bella rolled her eyes. "Perhaps I should not have said anything. This will only go straight to your head."

"I cannot deny it."

Bella laughed again. And again as the conversation went on as they talked and talked about Shakespeare and books and the little moments that had happened during the evening that they had both taken note of. By the end of it, her face hurt. Her cheeks remained flushed. Her empty glass had dried. When the time came for Lord Belmont to leave, taking the carriage offered by Gertrude since Lady Catherine had left in the other, Bella finally realized that their relationship had crossed over into unknown territory and she hadn't a clue how to navigate it.

Chapter Eighteen

Pain was often forgotten in the face of happiness. Finding pleasure in the mundane parts of life had seemed impossible for Edward after his mother passed, but somehow he'd made it there. He could laugh again, could share a drink with a friend without unloading the burden of his heartache, and looked forward to things once more. Edward didn't know when or how it happened. He supposed he could credit it all to time.

But the pain still lingered underneath it all and grew raw and throbbing like an open wound once faced with the cause of it all over again.

He stood before his mother's grave and thought back to the day she was buried. As a child, he hadn't known anything other than his tears and anger at the unfairness of the world. A beautiful, vibrant woman like his mother should have lived a long and happy life. To have it taken away from her, to have her taken away from him, felt like a cruel joke.

Now there were no tears. He simply fell, as he always did, into the past. Remembering how quickly she'd been mourned, how fast-paced her funeral had been. Now that he was older, he knew his father had only wanted to get it over with. The earl had always done what was expected of it him in the eyes of the ton and nothing more. He'd forced Edward to get over his grief as if it could possibly be that easy.

But then he remembered his mother's laughter, the passion in her voice as she told him stories of the past. Once upon a time, he'd believed that she'd truly lived in ancient Egypt or Mesopotamia or India. He soon understood that her love of history ran so deep that it was like she'd lived many lives before.

A calming wind brushed over the graveyard. It was located behind the parish church, which his mother frequented often when she was alive. Her grave had been kept clean and free of weeds, to his relief. Had it not been, he would have gotten on his knees and cleared the area himself. He would be quite a sorry sight when he arrived at the club later to see Luke.

What would she think of Isabella?

The question crossed his mind for a brief second before the answer came surging forward. His mother would have loved her. He hadn't a doubt that Isabella and she would have been kindred spirits and would easily form a friendship with or without his input. The thought brought a smile to his lips. He wished she could have met her.

He didn't know how long he stood there before he finally turned to leave. His joints ached as he made his way back to his waiting carriage. Even as the vehicle set off towards the club, his mind remained at the graveyard, the open wound of his ever-present grief slowly closing once more.

By the time he made it to the club, Edward felt more like himself. He found Luke already inside with a drink in his hand and his friend eagerly waved him over with a grin on his face.

"Come, come," Luke said as he approached. "I know you have much to tell me about your latest dealings with the love of your life."

Edward scowled at him as he slid into a chair. "Don't refer to our interactions as dealings. You make it sound so impersonal. And Lady Isabella is not the love of my life."

"I beg to differ," Luke said with a cheeky grin. "People are saying that you two look quite enamoured with each other."

"We are friends, nothing more. And what of you? It is high time you started taking your future a little more seriously."

Luke's brows shot upwards in surprise. "That is surprising coming from you. I almost thought it was the earl speaking to me just now."

"Coming from me, you should know it is out of concern and a selfish interest."

"I shall seek her soon enough. After I am finished living through you, of course." Luke leaned forward to whisper, "Are you certain you harbour no feelings for her?"

Edward hesitated. A 'no' should have rushed to his lips, but then he thought about what Amelia had said and the way he'd felt after responding to her. He didn't...did he?

"You look conflicted," Luke said. "Allow me to help you figure it out."

Edward gave him a skeptical look. "And what would you know about love?"

"You wound me, Edward! I know quite a bit. Just because I have not thought of settling down does not mean I do not know the nature of the heart. Now, let me ask you this. Do you think about her often when you are not around her?"

"Yes." *That* answer came quickly. So much so that it surprised him.

Luke only nodded as if he'd expected as much. "When you are with her, do you feel happy?"

"I do."

"Do you grow sad when the time comes for you two to part ways?"

"Yes."

"Does she make your heart skip a beat?"

"Quite often."

"How would you describe her in one word?"

That gave him pause. There were too many words to describe Isabella. Beautiful, intelligent, witty, bold.

Only one word captured it all, encapsulating how he felt whenever he had the pleasure of being in her presence. "Mesmerising."

Luke nodded. Then a slow grin stretched across his face. "Surely I do not have to spell it out for you?"

Edward hardly heard him. The revelation had been slow to come, he realized, but the signs had been there. He'd just been too dense to notice it. Now there was no denying that he had developed true feelings for Isabella.

Something twisted in his chest when he thought of how uncomfortable she'd been when they'd first discussed the details of the wedding. And the truce they'd made under the watchful eye of his family portrait. Lady Isabella did not want to marry him. She did not fancy him or love him. She was only interested in friendship to soothe the sting of being forced into marriage.

Would he able to make her fall for him?

***

She was reading Shakespeare. And enjoying it. Bella could not believe it.

Her voice echoed within the drawing room even as her aunt slumbered before the hearth. Bella would have stopped reading the moment she noticed her aunt had fallen asleep but she went on for some reason. Perhaps it had something to do with the electric pair of blue eyes that lingered in her mind.

She paused for a moment as the memory of Edward brought a smile to her lips. When would she see him again, she wondered. He had promised to take her to the museum and that was yet to happen. But if he was much a business man as his father was, she knew he didn't have much free time. It was likely that whatever social events he could attend were being taken up by his family and hers.

Even so, Bella longed to see him again. It had only been a day since she'd seen him last and she missed him dearly.

A knock on the door disrupted her thoughts. Bella closed the book and listened as the butler announced a visitor. Before she had the chance to inquire who it was, Lady Catherine breathed in.

"My lady!' Bella shot to her feet, remembering her manners a second later to curtsy. "What a…surprise. You did not send word that you would be visiting."

"I did not need to send word." Lady Catherine breezed past Bella and sat in her father's preferred armchair. She scanned the room with narrowed eyes and spotted Gertrude sleeping next to the hearth, Mr. Whiskers slumbering in her lap.

Bella felt a twist of anger at Lady Catherine's sneer. "Lady Wentworth?" she called, quietly of course. Bella knew her aunt wouldn't even stir at that. Lady Catherine cleared her throat she said a little louder, "Lady Wentworth!"

Only Mr. Whiskers opened his eyes and hissed loudly. Bella stifled a giggle.

Lady Catherine huffed in annoyance and turned back to face Bella. "A lady must conduct herself with dignity at all times. What is she doing?"

"I'm sure it offends no one if she sleeps in her own home, my lady," Bella couldn't resist saying. She met Lady Catherine's judgmental eyes without fear as she sat. "To what do I owe the pleasure?"

Lady Catherine said nothing for a moment as if deciding how best to respond. But then she snapped her fingers loudly. The door opened and Bella watched, appalled, as Annie entered the room bearing a box.

"Annie, what are you doing?" she asked her.

Annie bowed her head, not daring to meet her eyes. "Upon arrival, Lady Catherine requested a maid's assistance, my lady," she explained.

Bella bit her tongue to quell the irritation that surged in her, though it only succeeded in keeping her from lashing out. She did not appreciate Lady Catherine ordering her maid around in the slightest.

"Rest it there," Lady Catherine commanded with another snap. "And be quick about it!"

Annie hurried forward to set the box down on the table between Bella and Lady Catherine. Lady Catherine waved her hand. "Now begone."

Annie scurried out of the room. It took all of Bella's strength not to say anything.

"Go ahead," Lady Catherine urged. "I brought this for you."

At first, Bella didn't move. She reveled in the brief act of rebellion even though she knew it would do her no favors. Then she reached for the box and pulled out the dress that was folded within.

Bella couldn't believe her eyes, could not find the proper words. Finally, she settled on, "Is this...yours, my lady?"

Lady Catherine looked as pleased as Bella had ever seen. It was not a pretty sight. "*Was*," she emphasized. "And now it is yours. My kindness clearly knows no bounds. You should be grateful I am here to assist you."

"Assist me?" Bella was still too shocked to process what was being said to her.

Lady Catherine's ever-present sneer returned. "This will be the dress you wear to your engagement ball. I have saved you the trouble of seeking one yourself."

"Do you not think that I own any dresses of my own, my lady?"

"Pardon me?"

Bella swallowed, trying to maintain her composure. But the horror and frustration she felt threatened to overtake her. How could Lady Catherine ever think this was an appropriate thing to do? Not only was the dress so obviously altered by an inept modiste but the fashion and color was very outdated. No one in this day and age would consider wearing such a thing. To their engagement ball, no less!

"If I didn't know any better, Lady Isabella, I would think that you did not appreciate my kindness. Is this how your mother has been raising you?"

The mention of her mother nearly sent her over the edge. Bella didn't know how she held herself together. Her mother would not have allowed her to accept something like this. Anyone with eyes could see that Lady Catherine had pulled this from the back of her armoire and intended to pass it off as a gift.

Gertrude, on the other hand, deep in dreamland as she was, would urge her to accept. She would say that it was the polite thing to do. And her father would have her do anything that wouldn't jeopardize the arranged betrothal. Bella's hands were tied.

That was the only reason she forced a smile onto her face and said, "Thank you, Lady Catherine."

"You are welcome." She paused, looking at Bella expectantly. "Well, what are you waiting for? Go and try it on."

"Right now?"

"Yes, I would like to see it. I do not have all day."

Bella rose reluctantly. "I will return shortly then."

She left the room barely holding back the urge to toss the dress into the fire. That would certainly wake Gertrude.

Annie was lingering on the other side of the drawing room. She approached Bella, looking concerned. "She told me that I must stay nearby until she has left, in the case that I am needed."

"Of course, she did," Bella sighed. "She wishes for me to wear this horrid dress for my engagement ball and she will not leave until I have tried it."

"Oh dear," Annie murmured as she followed Bella up the steps.

"Annie, you should see it. It is such an insult. She may as well just come right out and say that she was making space in her armoire and did not want to throw it away."

"I'm sure it is not that bad, milady," Annie tried to console.

Bella scoffed. "You just wait and see then."

Annie was eating her words in the next half hour. It took them that long to squeeze Bella into the dress. It was incredibly tight and would have perfectly fit Lady Catherine's rail-thin physique. But since Bella held a little bit more weight, she had to hold her breath to keep from ripping the seams. Whatever alterations Lady Catherine had mentioned had clearly not been done with Bella in mind.

But that paled in comparison to the appearance of the dress itself. Bella could hardly look at herself. It was a frilly thing with too many layers of tulle under the skirt and sleeves that both capped and stretched to her wrists. The neckline touched the underside of her chin, the buttons almost as big as her palm. It was a horrible clash of red and blue as well. Bella didn't know why Lady Catherine had purchased it in the first place.

Annie could offer no more words of consolation and so they made their way back to the drawing room in silence. Lady Catherine was sipping tea inside, Gertrude still inside, and Mr. Whiskers watching everything in disapproval.

Lady Catherine studied Bella for a moment, sipping her tea. For a second, Bella thought she would come to her senses and realize what a horrible idea this all was. But she smiled instead, nodding. "Exactly as I predicted. You look lovely, Lady Isabella!"

"Do I?" Bella asked incredulous. She pressed her hands against the tulle-stuffed skirt. "You do not think it is a bit too…much?"

"Nonsense! You will stand out and that is what we want, isn't it? You cannot be seen as a wallflower at your own engagement ball. Again, you should thank me."

Bella couldn't force herself to say those words again. She stayed quiet, hands fidgeting behind her back. Lady Catherine nodded happily again and stood. She approached Bella, looking her up and down.

"You will have to pin all of your hair up," she stated, flicking the end of one of Bella's curls. "Proper footwear as well, though you will not dance."

"How can one not dance at their own ball?"

"Silence," the older woman hissed. She continued circling her. "No rouge, very little perfume, and no jewelry."

Bella's lips thinned into a straight line. She didn't bother to say that she had no intentions of listening to anything Lady Catherine had to say.

As if she sensed the direction of Bella's thoughts, Lady Catherine stopped directly in front of her and peered down her nose. "Do I make myself clear?"

"You do," Bella pushed through tight lips. *And it matters not to me.*

"Good." Lady Catherine turned her attention to Annie. "You are dismissed, maid. Stop lingering in conversation that does not involve you."

Annie bowed her head, muttered "Yes, my lady", and scampered away. It was all Bella could do to keep her simmering rage from boiling over.

"Is there anything else I can help you with, Lady Catherine?" Bella asked. And then, realizing that she might have left the question a little too open, she added, "If not, then I hope you will not mind if I retire to my chambers for a short rest. It has been a tiresome morning thus far."

"Like aunt, like niece, I suppose," Lady Catherine said, sending another scathing look in Gertrude's direction. Bella was honestly a little surprised that her aunt had slept through the entire thing. "Very well. There is nothing for me here."

Primly, Lady Catherine made her way to the door and Bella followed reluctantly. She would have liked to leave it up to the butler to escort her out but Bella didn't want to risk her accosting any more of the maids as she left. Thankfully, the short trek to the front door was uneventful and quiet. Lady Catherine only looked back at her once, from head to toe, then chuckled to herself before walking through the front door.

Bella stood by the window and watched as she climbed into her carriage. Mr. Whiskers trotted up behind her and hissed.

"I hate it too, Mr. Whiskers," Bella mumbled. The cat simply meowed balefully and wandered off.

Chapter Nineteen

The only thing that made visiting his father's home bearable was the chance of seeing Amelia. And it was a slim chance, Edward knew. Amelia, being the busy bee that she was, may very well be out socializing than indoors.

To Edward's pleasure, the butler informed him that Amelia was in the library. Edward headed straight there, going right by his father's office even though a summon from the earl was what brought him here in the first place. If he could delay seeing him as much as he could, he would.

Amelia sat in an armchair by the hearth with a book in her hand. She hummed as she read, tapping her fingers on the armrests.

"I cannot imagine how well you can focus while doing that," he commented and chuckled when she jumped.

"Edward!" Amelia gasped. "Don't you know it is very improper to sneak up on a lady like that?"

"Is it? I have never been taught such an obscure rule." He leaned against the hearth, crossing his arms. "Or are you just making things up so that I will feel guilty?"

"I would if I knew that it would work," she said with a roll of her eyes. Her smile came quickly after. "What are you doing here? Did you come to visit me?"

"I wish that were the case, but if I wished to see you I would simply invite you to my home instead. You know I prefer not to come here if I can help it."

Amelia's smile fell into a pout. "Did Father summon you then? I hope it isn't anything serious."

"It likely has something to do with business," Edward said dismissively.

"Or Lady Isabella," Amelia suggested. "You know he has not been able to talk about anything but that."

"Is that so?"

"I know you care very little for father's opinion but he seems quite pleased by the progression of everything. I would not be surprised if he called you over to say that."

"Such things could have easily been said in a letter."

Amelia sighed. "Goodness, while I do understand your reservations towards our father, Edward, I cannot help but think that you exacerbate it with your..."

"With my what?"

"Your...coldness. Is this how you are towards your betrothed?"

Not even a little bit, Edward almost said. His behavior towards Isabella was nothing but warm and gentle because that was the treatment she deserved. He could do so much more for her if she wished it.

But it was not knowing *if* she would wish it that gave him pause.

He didn't say that to Amelia but she smiled knowingly as if she understood all the words left unsaid. "I shan't keep you then," Amelia said, returning her attention to her book. "If you linger here any longer, I will only tease you and I doubt you will appreciate that."

"Tease all you wish, Amelia," Edward said. "But do not forget that I know your secret as well."

"My secret?"

"With your admirer." At her look of complete bemusement, he blinked. "Oh. Have you not received the letter then?"

Amelia shot out of the chair. "What letter?" she demanded.

Edward shook his head, trying his best not to laugh. "No, I cannot say. I have been sworn to secrecy."

"By whom?" As Edward began to walk away, Amelia seized his arm desperately. "Who swore you to secrecy, Edward?"

Edward sighed heavily then leaned closer to whisper, "I shan't say."

"Edward!"

His laughter rang out in the library. Amelia stomped her foot in frustration and the moment she let him go, he sauntered towards the door. He half-expected her to run after him and demand that he tell her what he knew—which was nothing—but when he looked back, she was only glaring at him. Edward laughed again and left the room.

His humor lingered all the way to the door of his father's study. When he knocked and his father called for him to enter, it fled completely.

As usual, Edward stayed by the door when he entered. Humphrey did not look up. He was writing furiously, so much so that Edward could see the whiteness of his knuckles from the distance. He said nothing, waiting for him to finish.

When he had finished, Humphrey tossed the quill pen into the nearby pot of ink and leaned back in the chair, pinching the bridge of his nose as if he was fighting the onset of a megrim.

"The quicker you tell me why you have asked me to come here, Father, the quicker I am able to leave," Edward said.

Humphrey scowled, finally giving Edward his attention. "Sit."

Edward remained where he was. Tense silence ensued for a few seconds before Humphrey sighed. "You look at me as if you expect me to send you off to war."

"You signed my life away and threatened my sister and my aunt to keep me in line," Edward drawled. "So I do not think that is very hard to imagine."

"Despite that, I am proud of you, Edward."

The tension that had sunken into Edward's shoulders tightened further at those words. Proud? Edward had never heard such a thing from his father.

"Come and have a seat, Edward," Humphrey urged, gentler this time.

And because he was still in shock, Edward moved without thinking. He sank into the armchair across from his father. Humphrey reached into the pocket of his tailcoat and pulled a handkerchief free. He coughed harshly into it, the sound a little concerning.

"As I was saying," Humphrey began again when the coughing fit was over. "I was expecting more of a fight about this matter. But you have played your part and truly shown maturity in accepting your position."

"Surely you are not praising me for falling for your blackmail, Father?"

"Do not think of it that way. Consider instead the benefit the entire family will see as a result of your union with Lady Isabella. Your sister and aunt will thank you for it."

"Your daughter and your sister should not have to worry about their lives being torn apart because of my decision."

Humphrey frowned. "I called you here because I wanted to commend you on all that you have done, Edward. There is no reason for this to turn into an argument."

His mother would have argued. She always did. Even when his father grew aggressive, she never backed down, even when she did temporarily withdraw. Edward had adopted her fire and he would be damned if he'd let his father stomp it out of him.

"The engagement ball is this evening, is it not?" Humphrey asked. "Catherine tells me that the details have all been finalized and that it is only a matter of attending at this point."

"Yes, that is so." Edward couldn't care less about the ball. He was only going along with it because it was another chance to see Isabella.

And, though he wouldn't dare to admit it aloud, he was now looking forward to flaunting Lady Isabella on his arm as his own. Even if she, deep down, did not wish it to be so.

"Good. Be prepared. I have a few acquaintances who will be attending and they..."

Edward stopped listening. He should have known what this was truly about. His father did not usher kind or encouraging words unless it suited him. And of course, this ball was only going to benefit him in the end. He'd only called Edward here to make sure that he fell in line with his plans.

Instead of listening, Edward focused on the only bright spot of the evening. Seeing Isabella again.

***

"Annie, I cannot attend wearing that. I simply cannot."

The distress on Annie's face was enough to distract Bella from her own for a brief moment. "But won't Lady Catherine be upset if you do not?"

"I care not what Lady Catherine thinks!" Bella stated strongly, even though she was well aware that that was a lie. Caring about what Lady Catherine thought, however reluctantly, was what had put her in this predicament in the first place.

Bella flopped onto her bed with a heavy sigh, staring up at the ceiling. A few minutes ago, she had held stalwart in her rebellion. She would not wear the dress, no matter what might happen when Lady Catherine saw her later this evening. She'd decided that she wouldn't care about the older woman's opinion nearly as much as everyone wanted her to.

That was what she wanted to do, in her heart of hearts. The actual execution, however, was a little difficult to follow through with. Now that the time came to actually get dressed, the consequences of her actions weighed heavily on her. If she wore the dress, she would be a spectacle of humiliation that would be talked about for years to come.

Do you remember the dress Lady Isabella wore to her own engagement ball? Hasn't she any shame?

The thought alone made her insides curl in on itself. The alternative however was defying Lady Catherine and risking her wrath. Which would in turn backfire on Bella if Lady Catherine said the wrong thing to her father. Victor would surely make her regret ever attempting to defy her in the first place. Heavens, he might lock her away until the day of her wedding this time!

Conflicted, Bella closed her eyes. She could all but feel Annie's anxiety as the maid hovered near the bed and wrung her hands together.

"Perhaps we could alter it a bit ourselves?" Annie suggested.

Bella sighed. "A fine idea, Annie but we haven't the time for that now."

"Then, and forgive me if this seems a little outrageous milady, but if you do not wish to wear the dress then maybe you could feign illness and..." Annie didn't finish the sentence. Bella considered it for a moment then shook her head.

"Father will be furious. I will have to put on quite the act if I hope of receiving any sympathy or understanding."

There was nothing she could do. Bella was completely out of options.

There came a knock on her door. Bella quickly got to her feet as she said, "Yes?"

Gertrude entered with a maid walking in behind. She looked Bella up and down and asked, "Why aren't you dressed yet? It is almost time to leave."

"I..." Gertrude hadn't seen the dress. Bella had informed her of what transpired while she'd napped but hadn't been able to pull the horrid dress out of her armoire to show her. She'd hoped that, after tucking it to the very back, it would magically disappear somehow.

"I will be donning my dress now, Aunt," Bella said reluctantly.

"No need to," Gertrude said dismissively. "I suppose I should be happy for your laziness this time since it might save us time. I wanted to give you this earlier but did not find the time."

She waved the maid forward. Bella was struck with a heavy dose of deja vu as the maid came forward bearing a box. Only this time the dress laid within was the most beautiful article of clothing Bella had ever seen.

It was a subtle shade of her favorite color: green. The design was simple yet fashionable, with a lowered neckline overlayed with lace. There was only one layer of tulle under the dress, enough to give it shape but not overwhelm her own figure. The sleeves were capped and she could already imagine pairing it with a lovely pair of gloves she already possessed.

It was beautiful. And perfect for her.

"Aunt Gertrude..." she whispered in awe, pulling it free. "How did you..."

"Worry not about the details," her aunt said. "You should hurry and get dressed before we are late—"

Bella threw her arms around her aunt, catching the older woman by surprise. She knew. Gertrude understood and had hoped to save her from embarrassment without saying anything about it.

"Thank you," she breathed before stepping away. So moved, Bella had to blink her tears away.

Gertrude looked a little taken aback by Bella's show of affection. For a moment, Bella thought she might crack but then she straightened and said, "You're welcome. Now, hurry I said."

"Yes, madam!"

Bella grinned as she watched her aunt leave the room. Then the turned to face Annie, who was wiping tears from the corner of her eyes. "Our prayers have been answered, Annie," Bella stated happily.

"Thank heavens for that, milady," Annie responded with a smile.

Chapter Twenty

Edward had to admit, his aunt had outdone herself.

The ballroom had been transformed, opulence dripping from every corner as if she had not bothered to spare a single expense. Every guest that stepped through the door was awed by the shimmering, albeit a bit overbearing, chandeliers, the glistening floors, the ornate chairs placed throughout the large interconnected room. Praises about the decorations poured from all the lips that went by them until Edward had fallen into a routine of saying, "Thank you. Please, it is Lady Catherine who deserved the praise".

It had been nearly an hour of this while the ball steadily grew fuller and fuller. Of course, his father was not here to issue greetings to the guests, no doubt thinking he had better things to do. So it was Catherine, Amelia and him standing near the entrance, bowing and curtsying and greeting everyone who went by.

Edward would have abandoned this task long ago, of course. But he was waiting on a certain lady to arrive. Until then, he planned on staying right where he was.

"You look terribly uninterested in being here." Luke seemed to appear out of nowhere. Before Edward could stop him, the viscount pinched Edward's cheek, pulling them apart. "Smile, Edward! This is your ball!"

"Let go of me or I shall have you kicked out," Edward growled, slapping Luke's hands away. Amelia giggled next to him.

"Lord Fellington," she greeted, sinking into a curtsy. "It has been a while since we've seen each other last, has it not?"

"Do not tell me this is little Amelia?" Luke asked with exaggeratingly large eyes. "You seem to have shot up overnight! The last I saw you, you were just a little girl!"

"I think your memory is failing you, my lord," Amelia teased.

"Perhaps you are right. It may take some time to refresh it. Why don't we do so over the first dance? It is the waltz, I presume?"

That last question was aimed at Edward who nodded in surprise. He watched as Luke stepped forward to scribble his name on Amelia's dance card, while she blushed.

"I shall find you, my lady," Luke said as he stepped back.

"I should hope that you do, my lord," Amelia responded.

Edward remained quiet as his friend gave him a nod of farewell and then sauntered deeper into the ball to socialize with others. They'd been flirting with each other, he realized a moment too late. Something about that made him uneasy.

"Is he the one sending the letter?" Amelia whispered to him. "I know he is your only friend so it would only make sense."

"No," Edward answered curtly. "There will be no letter. I was only jesting."

"Goodness, I hate you," Amelia whispered, though she did not sound that annoyed. Perhaps she had already suspected as much.

Edward nudged her playfully and she nudged him back. He was tempted to tell her that he loved her, that as his younger sister, he was both looking forward to and dreading the day she debuted. All those words melted to the back of his throat when he noticed Thomas approaching.

He leaned in to greet Catherine first, who accepted his affection primly. She had been the one mainly greeting the guests while Edward and Amelia were distracted but now her attention was focused solely on her nephew.

"You are early," she commented. "No one has arrived yet."

An odd comment to make seeing that the ballroom was nearly full. Thomas grinned. "Worry not, Aunt. I shan't give you any trouble. Yet." He winked and Catherine only rolled her eyes.

Edward couldn't understand her softness towards him. He was a known troublemaker who contributed little to the family and was always on the verge of bringing scandal to her late husband's name. Thomas went against everything Catherine stood for.

Perhaps it was because he was family, though it was only by name. Or perhaps she saw something in him that no one else could.

Edward could see how charming Thomas could be, but that was not enough to make his personality any easier to stomach. In his opinion, at least. It took all he could not to simply walk away when Thomas turned his attention to him.

"I do not think I have congratulated you, cousin," Thomas said.

Edward gritted his teeth. "There is no need," he pushed through.

"Of course, there is. You have managed to secure a betrothal with a beautiful young lady who nearly every other gentleman present would have loved to have as his own. You are the object of envy, I'm sure you know."

"It matters not to me what others think, Thomas."

"I can see that." That easy grin on Thomas' lips did not touch his eyes completely. "Though I must wonder how much of your union is genuine."

"Thomas..." Catherine called in a warning tone.

But everyone ignored her. Edward narrowed his eyes at Thomas, pulling his shoulders back as if gearing up for a fight. Thomas raised his chin, that smirk on his face inciting a level of anger in Edward that he could hardly contain.

"What are you trying to say, Thomas?" Edward asked as calmly as he could.

"Nothing, really," Thomas responded with a shrug. "I only wonder if your future union is made out of true affection for each other or yet another business transaction your family and you are renown for."

"I do not see how that is any of your concern."

"It is not, I suppose. I only speak out of worry."

"For whom? Yourself?"

"Lady Isabella." His smirk widened. "She seems like such a wonderful person. I would hate for her to sign her life away to a man who will not care for her the way that she deserves."

Edward approached slowly until the tips of his toes touched Thomas'. "I will only say this once, Thomas. Lady Isabella's and my relationship is none of your concern. You'd best turn your attention to other things."

Thomas tilted his head to the side, eyes darkening. "Or what?"

"Aunt," Edward heard Amelia whisper behind him. "Won't you stop them?"

Catherine sighed heavily. She placed a bony hand on Edward's shoulder and squeezed. "All right, enough. You two are causing a scene."

That was almost true. Others were looking, the nosiest of guests drifting closer to overhear what was being said. Edward forced himself to step back even though the only thing he wanted to do was tackle Thomas to the ground.

"Don't mind me, cousin," Thomas said easily. "I am but a concerned family member, after all."

Edward didn't dare to respond, knowing that whatever came out of his mouth would be nothing good and would likely make things worse.

Suddenly, the air shifted. The tension dissipated as everyone's attention turned towards the entrance. Edward did the same and the anger that had been threatening to overflow now faded into nothing.

Isabella had arrived. Her aunt and father stood by her side as well but Edward—and he suspected everyone else nearby—only had eyes for her. She had always been beautiful but this evening, there were no words to describe what he thought of her. Stunning did not have enough impact, his previous description using the word mesmerizing was not nearly strong enough.

The only thing he could say for certain was that she had stolen his breath away.

Lady Isabella walked forward with the grace of a queen, eyes trained ahead. Lady Wentworth greeted others as they drew closer and the duke's hard expression did not lift for a second. Edward swallowed, taking a step back as they approached because he wasn't certain he'd be capable of proper words just yet.

"What is she wearing?" Catherine hissed. "That is not the dress I gave her."

"I think she looks lovely," Amelia commented. "She truly is the belle of the ball. Isn't she, Edward?"

Edward nodded, still incapable of words. They were almost upon them and he was no closer to bringing himself back to life.

At last, the family stopped before them. Lady Wentworth and Isabella sank into curtsies while the duke simply dipped his head in a shadow of a bow. "Good evening, my ladies, my lord," Lady Wentworth started. "I must say that I am rather impressed by the decorations."

Edward didn't listen to the pleasantries. His eyes met Isabella's and his heart restarted in his chest.

"My lady, you look...breathtaking," he breathed, not caring that others were close enough to overhear them. He didn't even care about the fact that Thomas was still lingering, his sly eyes taking everything in.

Pink tinged her cheeks as she smiled. "Thank you, my lord."

Edward wanted to say so many other things all of a sudden. His mind raced with the possibilities of different conversations but his first task was to secure his spot as her first dance partner.

"May I?" he asked, gesturing to the dance card already tied to her wrist.

Isabella seemed bemused for a moment then she nodded as a knowing smile stretched across her lips. "Certainly, my lord."

He stepped closer, inhaling the subtle scent of lavender that wafted from her skin. His hand shook a little as he wrote his name. Edward couldn't believe that he had turned into this nervous shell of his former self in the face of love.

"My lady." Catherine's sharp voice cut through their little bubble. Isabella turned to face her. "That is not the gown I brought for you to wear."

Catherine sounded upset at that but Isabella did not look perturbed by it. "It is not, my lady. I was given this dress by my aunt and chose to wear it instead. I hope you do not mind the decision."

Catherine's face grew red with her apparent anger but before she could say anything, Lady Wentworth stepped in. "Do not worry about what she wears, my lady. I had grown sentimental while viewing the dress and thought that it would be a lovely gift for her before she went into matrimony. Don't you think she looks lovely?" She did not give Catherine a chance to answer that before she moved on. "Anyhow, we are missing the ball by standing here. Thank you again for planning this evening, my lady, and please, pass on our thanks to Lord Harenwood for hosting."

With that said, Lady Wentworth slipped her arm through Isabella's and steered her deeper into the ball. Isabella gave Edward a lingering glance before she allowed herself to be whisked away. Edward stared after her, not caring who was looking.

Thomas decided that was the right moment to remind everyone that he was still standing there. "What an interesting sight," he commented vaguely. "I think I may enjoy this ball after all."

He didn't linger for a response, walking off with his hands tucked in his pockets. Edward tried to quell the surge of uneasiness he felt at those words.

Chapter Twenty-One

Bella was tapping her foot and Gertrude was far too close to snapping at her for it. But she could not help herself. She was excited, humming with eagerness for the first set to begin. She kept looking at Lord Belmont's name written on her dance card and could not contain the impatience she felt that the time to dance was not now.

"I am a fool, Isabella," Eleanor sighed beside her. It distracted Bella momentarily from her own thoughts.

Bella followed Eleanor's line of sight and giggled. "You are not a fool, Eleanor. You are simply too kind for your own good."

Eleanor did not seem comforted by those words. She sighed dramatically and buried her face in her gloved hands, earning a look from Gertrude. "Even so, I should have known better than to give in to Lord Bale's request. Now he will hound me to the ends of the earth."

Bella couldn't help but laugh even though she sympathized with her friend. Lord Bale had been enamored with Eleanor from the moment she debuted. He was a young lord with unfortunate premature balding and a penchant for talking about himself for hours. No matter how many love letters, flowers, and other gifts he tried to shower Eleanor in, she would always reject his advances. Even so, Lord Bale was a persistent man. Bella knew that it was only a matter of time before he wore Eleanor down.

"There is nothing I can do to stop this," Eleanor complained. "I am doomed."

"It is only one dance," Bella tried to say but Eleanor was already shaking her head.

"It is never only just one dance. You know that as well as I do."

Bella couldn't deny that. Lord Bale would attach himself to Eleanor's side. If it weren't for the fact that she always looked completely put off by his presence—evident to everyone except the lord himself—rumors about their courtship would have certainly begun.

Bella tried to think of some other way to console her friend but the chance was gone the moment the orchestra began. The first set for the night was about to commence. While Eleanor's shoulders sank in defeat, Bella's heart began to race, her eyes skimming through the crowd for the familiar head of dark hair.

Instead, it was Lord Granville who appeared before her, blocking her view.

"My lady," he greeted. "I did not get the chance to tell you earlier how beautiful you looked."

"Thank you, my lord." Bella tried not to seem impatient, her politeness just barely slipping through her teeth.

"If I was not already aware of your betrothal to my cousin, perhaps I would have taken a chance at winning your heart myself."

The words were bold, bold enough for Gertrude to take notice and give her a warning glance. Bella knew she had to tread carefully. "Your words flatter me, my lord."

"Shall I have the honour of this dance then?"

"I have already promised the first dance to my betrothed, my lord."

"Surely he will not mind? I do not see him anywhere, do you?" Lord Granville made a show of looking around before turning his smirk to her. "All right, I shan't step on his toes. But perhaps you will save time for me later?"

"Do you mean another dance, Lord Granville?" she asked carefully. "If so, I am free after a few more sets if you wish to write your name on my dance card."

"Yes." His grin was wide, eyes sparkling with humor she did not quite understand. "Yes. Another dance. That is exactly what I mean."

He held out his hand. Bella hesitated. There was something about the way he looked at her that made her wonder if it was a good idea. But then a large hand seized Lord Granville's, forcing it back to his side. Bella let out a silent breath of relief when Lord Belmont stepped in between them.

She expected him to say something to Lord Granville but he only glared at him for a few seconds before turning to her. "The set is about to start," he said softly to her. "Shall we?"

Bella placed her hand in his and fought the urge to grin madly. "Yes, certainly, my lord."

She barely spared Lord Granville another glance as they made their way to the center of the room. The first dance would be the waltz. An intimate dance that made her wonder just how clearly Lord Belmont could hear the pounding of her heart. Butterflies erupted in her stomach when he pulled her closer and placed his hand on the small of her back, splaying his fingers.

"You should be careful of him," he murmured to her as they began the slow steps back and forth.

"Why?" Bella asked curiously.

"Because I know him far better than you do. He hasn't said or done anything yet but he shall." At her silence, he looked down at her with a frown. "Or has he already?"

Bella mulled over how honest she should be right now even as the truth rushed to the tip of her tongue. She settled on half-truths, not wanting to overstep. "Lord Granville is charming...in his own way though I will heed your warning since you've deigned to give it. To be honest I did not expect our first discussion for the evening to begin with him."

"Oh?" Mirth lined his voice. "Have you given it much thought, my lady?"

"Please, call me Isabella," she said boldly. "Or Bella, as everyone else does. I think it is only proper at this point."

He squeezed her hand. He began stroking his thumb back and forth against her back. It sent shivers throughout her body. "Isabella," he purred. "You have such a beautiful name. It fits you perfectly."

She hid her face against his shoulder to hide her blush. "It is my late grandmother's name on my mother's side. I could not decide if their decision was sweet or lazy."

"Perhaps a bit of both?" Edward suggested with a chuckle. "Though I do find it quite interesting that we have yet another thing in common. My name hails from my mother's father. Edwin was his name."

"Did you ever get to meet him?" Bella asked softly. "Your grandfather."

"I did though my memory of him is quite hazy. I was young, you see. And he was nearing the death bed. But I do know that my mother was quite close to him."

"I'm sure he cherished the time he spent with you."

"That is what my mother liked to say as well."

Bella didn't miss the thread of sadness in his voice, even though he didn't break rhythm. He swept her in circles, their steps matching perfectly even though both their minds were so far from here. Talking about their parents reminded her what she had and of what she didn't. Her mother and sister should have been here with her. But Edward...he had no one but himself. His sister had him but who did he have to rely on?

She wished she could stay a little longer, just to console him with her presence since she could not find the right words. But the dance would not last forever, no matter how much she wanted it to.

When they stepped away from each other, Bella had to fight every urge in her body to step back into his embrace. Edward looked conflicted, as if he was fighting the same thing.

"Would you like for me to fetch you a glass of lemonade, Isabella?"

Her name on his lips was enough to make her entire body grow hot. Bella nodded wordlessly, not trusting herself to speak just yet. He nodded and eagerly set off in the direction of the refreshments table.

Bella stepped back, out of the way of the other retreating dancers but still in the same area so that Edward could find her again. While she waited, she looked through the crowd of people and spotted Lord Bale following desperately after Eleanor as she tried her hardest to escape him.

"All alone again, my lady?"

Bella nearly groaned aloud. She didn't look up as Lord Granville stopped by her side. "So it would seem, my lord," she answered in a dry tone.

"Well pardon me if I seem a little forward but I am here to request another dance. There is something I wished to speak with you about."

The seriousness of his words seemed a little out of place for him. Bella looked up at him and that usual smirk on his face was barely there. He held out a hand. "I shall return you to your betrothed as soon as I am finished."

Curiosity got the best of her. Bella glanced in the direction of the refreshments table and was just barely able to make out Edward's head above the rest. Perhaps, had she not been waiting on him, she might have given in to the curiosity. Perhaps she would have let Lord Granville lure her into the dance floor. But she did not want to keep Edward waiting.

"It may be serious, but I doubt that it is urgent, my lord," Bella said firmly. "If you do not mind, perhaps we could have this conversation later."

Lord Granville's hand fell and he let out a long breath. "You are as insolent as my aunt says you are."

"Pardon me?"

"Follow me, my lady, or else there will be consequences you will not want on your conscience." He stepped closer, pointing in the direction Eleanor and Lord Bale had disappeared. He'd cornered her at the back of the ballroom now. Though she looked uncomfortable, it didn't look as if he was doing anything untoward.

Yet.

The implication of Lord Granville's words settled like cold ice on Bella's chest. She slid a glare at him. "You would not dare."

He shrugged. "Lord Bale owes me quite a lot, my lady. And I found it quite easy to persuade him seeing that he's already had an interest in Lady Eleanor in the first place. Now, shall we?"

Without waiting for a response, he turned and walked away. Bella stared after him, hands turned into fists at her side. She looked back at the refreshments table and saw that Edward was making his way back to her.

She turned and followed.

Lord Granville kept his pace and so she fell far behind, though she kept him in her sights. She didn't want anyone to think she was actually following him. When he went past the doors and out into the garden, Bella hesitated.

He wouldn't dare to lead her deep into the garden, would he?

This was a bad idea. She knew it even as she kept course. Even as she brushed past the doors and her cool night breeze settled over her, Bella continued. She thought of Eleanor and grew afraid of what might happen if she didn't. Bella knew very well that the ton cared little for a gentleman's reputation as they did a lady's. It wouldn't matter if Eleanor was not at fault. No one could care except Bella.

She stopped when she was a few feet away from the doors, far enough to hear herself speak clearly but close enough for her to see what was going on inside. "Stop," she called.

Lord Granville paused and turned to look at her.

"I shall go no further," she stated. "Speak your mind so that this may be over with."

"Perhaps we could go—"

"No." Bella shook her head and crossed her arms. "Now speak."

In the darkness, she saw his smirk. Slowly began to walk towards her. The closer he came, the more she realized that the smirk was more akin to a sneer. "Lady Isabella," he purred. "You should be much kinder to the men around you. To think I was trying to help you."

"Help me by doing what?" she couldn't help but ask even as she felt a shimmer of fear run down her spine.

"It is about your betrothed," he said, sticking his hands in his pockets. "Surely you do not think he is a right match for you."

"I do not understand how that is any of your concern," Bella said stiffly. "But if you must know, Edward's and my betrothal was arranged by our fathers. I had no more say in the matter as he did."

"Is that what he led you to believe?" Lord Granville tilted his head back and laughed. Then he came closer, far too close for her comfort. Bella took a step back. "If that is what you wish to believe then I shan't be the one to tell you the truth."

"Then it seems we are done here." She turned to leave but he seized her wrist so tightly that pain shot up her arm. Bella looked at him in alarm. "You are hurting me, my lord."

Lord Granville tugged her closer to him. Bella fought against his hold but, despite his lanky physique, he was quite strong. "Why don't I show you how good it can be before you marry?" he whispered to her.

Revulsion rushed up her throat. Bella continued to fight. "Let go of me or else I'll scream."

"Will you? And risk everyone knowing what is happening here?"

"There is *nothing* happening here," she insisted even as she tried pushing him away from her. All that it did was inspire him to wrap his arm around her waist and pull her to his chest.

"Oh, I beg to differ," he hummed as he buried his face in the crook of her neck.

Bella wanted to scream. The urge to do so built in her throat as she thrashed. He was strong enough to keep her pinned, horror spreading throughout her veins. The very thing she'd feared happening to Eleanor was about to happen to her.

"What is happening here?"

The exclamation was so loud that Bella almost didn't hear the chorus of gasps that sounded at the same time. Lord Granville pushed her away so forcefully that she nearly tripped over her feet. She righted herself in time but didn't dare turn right away.

She recognized the voice. It was the last person she'd ever wanted to see such a thing.

But Lady Catherine would not let her go easily. Bella sensed her approach with her back turned.

"My lady, are you out of your mind?" Lady Catherine demanded to know, far too loud and shrill for Bella's liking. She could hear whispers behind her. A crowd was gathering to witness the ruination of her reputation.

Swallowing and fighting the tears, she turned to face Lady Catherine, not daring to look at the people behind her. "It is not what you think," she said to her, though she made sure she spoke loud enough for others to hear. "Lord Granville was taking advantage of—"

"Don't you dare lie!" she screeched. "I saw you follow him out here. Did you think you were being discreet in your rendezvous?"

"This is not a rendezvous," Bella insisted, tears burning the back of her throat. She glanced at Lord Granville but he clearly had no intentions of coming to her defense. "As I said, it is not what it looks like."

"Then what is it, Isabella?"

Bella's heart stopped in her chest. She forced herself to look past Lady Catherine to the man pushing his way to the front. The look on Edward's face...it was enough to terrify and sadden her at the same time.

"Did you follow him out here like my aunt said?" Edward asked slowly, his eyes darker than she'd ever seen them.

She wanted to lie. But she relied on the truth instead, even though she knew it would only make things worse. "I did," she confessed. "But only because he said he had something important to tell me."

"And whatever that was could not be said with others present?" Edward asked incredulously.

Bella knew how foolish it sounded. Heavens, she knew how foolish it was while she was doing it! But the threat that had loomed over Eleanor's head had been her only motivation.

She couldn't say that, she knew. Even when she met Eleanor's worried eyes in the crowd, Bella knew she had to keep that tidbit of truth to herself.

Before she could say anything, her father and aunt rushed forward. "Bella, what is the meaning of this?" Victor demanded.

Bella didn't look at him. She should be afraid of what her father would do now that her reputation was in tatters but she could only focus on Edward, on the betrayal in his eyes.

"Bella." Her aunt took her hand, shielding her from the others. "Are you all right? Did he hurt you?"

Wordlessly, she shook her head. Her tears spilled over her cheeks. "It really isn't what you think," she murmured.

"Enough!" her father bellowed to everyone else. "There is nothing to see here. Go on, you all."

Only a few people meandered away. Eleanor, Amelia, Lady Catherine, Lord Granville, and Edward remained, as well as a few of the more nosy members of the ton.

"Isabella." Bella looked back at Edward. "The truth. Please."

That last word broke her into a million pieces. Because she couldn't. She couldn't tell the truth.

She clearly took too long to respond because Edward's expression changed. He grew cold, glaring at her as if she was nothing more than the dirt under her shoe. "Consider this betrothal void, my lady," he stated. "I shall not be married to a woman who throws herself at other gentlemen and then lie about it."

He didn't give her the chance to respond. Bella wasn't sure if that was a good thing or not. He stalked off, leaving everyone staring after him.

Eleanor rushed forward the moment he did but Victor seized Bella's upper arm so roughly that she was certain she would bruise. He pulled her away from everyone muttering, "We are leaving," in her ear. Bella didn't have the strength to fight back. She let him drag her along because she could hardly see with the tears clouding her eyes.

She didn't see when Eleanor tried to follow but Gertrude warned her to stay. She didn't see the eyes that trailed after them as they made their embarrassing trek through the ballroom to head back outdoors. And she certainly didn't see the smirk of satisfaction that had lifted Lady Catherine's lips.

Chapter Twenty-Two

He left the ball nearly immediately. It was a joke, he realized, to continue celebrating a betrothal that was no longer present. He locked himself in his old study, poured himself a glass of brandy, and tried to drown out the pain and sorrow that assaulted him.

Hours went by. The ball slowly trickled to an end, since everyone had seemed to content to continue without their presence. Or perhaps they were all just glad to be in one room where they could go from group to group gossiping about the latest scandal. In the midst of his bitterness and pain, Edward wished he could send them all home himself.

Soon enough, he no longer heard the music. Amelia found him after a while and begged him to let her in, but sent her away each time she came. Soon enough, she stopped. Catherine didn't bother to at all. Edward wondered if she was secretly pleased that this had all come to an end. He wondered if she cared that it felt as if his heart had been ripped out of his chest and stomped on by Isabella's slipper-clad feet.

He could not get the image of the two of them out of his mind. Edward stood and paced, pouring glass after glass until the decanter was empty and his mind was nothing but a fog. Even so, it did not help him forget the look on her face when he demanded to know the truth. He supposed there was some luck in having arrived late, seconds after they had been discovered. If he had actually seen them in the act, he might have done something utterly foolish.

What he'd seen had been enough to tear him into a million pieces, however. She'd lied to him, right to his face. And Thomas had stood behind her with that infernal smirk of his as if he expected her to protect him. Even though she said it was not what he thought, why couldn't she tell him what it truly was? Why couldn't she have revealed the truth if she wanted to be believed.

He didn't cry, not until the manor fully fell quiet. Not until he realized he had spent hours thinking about all that had transpired, the alcohol failing to chase his memory away. Tears stained his cheeks as he closed his eyes and let his exhaustion overtake him.

Sleep gave him no relief however. All he could see was Isabella and the pain of her betrayal standing between them.

The special license he'd obtained seemed to burn right through to his skin.

***

Bella threw herself onto her bed and let the tears consume her. She bawled loudly enough to send Gertrude away from her door when she came to inquire about her well-being. Her aunt hadn't gotten the chance to say anything since the entire carriage ride home had been spent listening to Victor berate her for how foolish she was. He'd criticized and shouted and called her useless a number of times but Bella did not feel the usual sting of his harsh words. She had been trying to hold herself together the entire time.

Now she let it all out, soaking her pillows. She cried until she was all out of tears and could only heave painfully at the slow tearing of her heart. Long after, her body would simply shake as she stared up at the ceiling and thought about what happened over and over again.

She loved him.

That was what scared her the most about all of this. How late her revelation was. She'd fallen deeply in love with Edward and she would never get the chance to say the words to him. She would never get to see his smile, to hear his warm voice, to listen to his laughter. She'd made sure of that this evening.

How could she have been so foolish?

Bella wished she had the strength to continue crying. At least that way she was a little distracted from the painful memory of how everything had come crashing down around her.

A knock sounded on the door. Bella didn't move. She expected whomever it was on the other end to knock a few more times and then go away but the door opened instead. "Milady?"

Annie's voice was so steeped in worry that it nearly stirred Bella back to life. She didn't move though. She continued staring up at the ceiling and prayed for sleep to claim her.

"'Milady, my apologies for entering without your permission," Annie said softly, staying by the door. "I have been standing outside your door for some time wondering if I should come in. I heard your crying and I..."

Bella didn't respond. She didn't think her throat was capable of speech after her painful wails earlier.

"I'm sorry, milady." Annie sounded like she was on the verge of tears herself. "I do not know what happened but I am so, so sorry that it did."

Somehow, that brought back the tears Bella thought had been emptied. She shifted into an upright position, her hair tumbling around her face. Goodness, her head hurt. "Annie, I do not know what to do."

"What happened, Lady Isabella?" Annie flew to her side in a second. She even sat on the edge of the bed, taking Bella's hand in hers. Her concern for Bella must have outweighed her position as a maid.

Bella turned her teary eyes to her and it all came rushing out of her. The truth the way she understood it. She needed to tell someone, someone she knew would not judge her or question her decisions, or make her feel guilty. Annie listened intently to it all though her eyes grew wider and wider in horror as Bella explained what nearly transpired between Lord Granville and her.

"I do not know what to do, Annie," Bella repeated once she was done. "Edward hates me, I have brought shame to my father's name, and he will certainly make sure that I suffer for it." She paused. Saying it aloud brought home the consequences of what had happened. "Edward hates me, Annie. You should have seen the look he gave me as he ended our engagement."

"Milady, you have been through so much in just one evening," Annie lamented softly. "I wish I knew the words to make you feel better."

"I will never feel better knowing that Edward will continue to think that I am nothing but a dishonourable woman. He has made it clear that he does not like Lord Granville. I'm sure he feels even stronger about the situation because of that." Bella sighed heavily, wiping her tears. Her eyes had swollen to the point that it obscured her vision and her face was so hot that she didn't need a mirror to know that her cheeks were as red as tomatoes.

"I cannot stay in London," she said without thinking.

"If only it were that simply, milady," Annie responded softly.

Bella shook her head. "It can be that simple. How can I remain here knowing that my life has fallen into pieces in mere hours? I cannot show my face in public again. I cannot face Edward. And I shudder to think what my father will do when the morning comes. No, I cannot stay here."

Annie got to her feet, looking horrified as Bella crawled out of the bed. "You aren't truly thinking of leaving, are you?"

"I am." Determination surged within her and Bella seized it like a starving woman. She clung to it, letting it numb the pain and sadness. "Help me back a satchel, Annie. We leave tonight."

"Milady, you cannot!"

"I can and I will. I will go to mother. She will know what to do." Bella hurried to her table, glancing back once to see that Annie was still frozen to the spot. "Pack my bags while I write a letter explaining where I have gone. Hopefully by the time anyone finds it I will be long gone. Far enough that they will not come after me."

Annie slowly got into motion and so Bella turned her attention to her table. She reached for a clean sheet of paper, her quill, and her ink and quickly wrote a letter to Gertrude. She made it short, explaining that the situation had escalated out of her control and she needed some reprieve to it all. She hoped that the letter would be enough to ease the worry she would leave behind when she was discovered missing.

Despite her obvious reservations, Annie moved quickly and effectively. She packed a satchel with Bella's undergarments, shoes, bonnets and a few dresses that should be enough to last the trip. Annie made sure to state aloud that she did not think this was a good idea while stripped her dress off and donned something more discreet. Bella ignored her warnings. She'd already decided that this was the best course of action. She was not running. Only retreating.

The house was quiet when they slipped out of their room. Annie led her towards the back, through the kitchen, and out into the vegetable gardens. They didn't bother to take a horse, delving down a beaten path that would lead them to the street. It was quite late at night, a heavy fog making it difficult for the light of the street lanterns to pass through. Bella clutched the reticule she'd brought with her close to her chest and prayed a stagecoach would go by.

She didn't have to pray long, thankfully. She let Annie do most of the talking, hoping that it would help them get a better price for the trip. Bella knew that the moment the coachman realized that she was a noble, his price may triple. She had saved a lot from her allowances over years but she didn't know if it would last, so she wanted to be careful.

Soon enough, the stagecoach set off in the direction of the countryside. Bella didn't release the breath she was holding until they reached the outskirts of London, far enough away that she was certain she'd pulled it off. She settled into the uncomfortable carriage as best as she could, pulled her cloak around her body, and tried to relax.

Running away wasn't going to help, she realized after a long while. Edward's eyes filled with betrayal would follow her to the end of the earth.

Chapter Twenty-Three

Sunlight burned the back of Bella's eyelids, willing her to open them. She peeled the back, breaking the layer of crust that had settled over them during the night. The first thing she noticed was that she was still so heavily exhausted that it would likely take days for her to feel like herself again. The second thing was that she was not in her bedchamber.

All of last night's happenings hit her like a runaway horse. Bella closed her eyes briefly, willing the images—and the pain—away. But they consumed her instead and she was forced to relive it all.

Slowly, she sat up. Annie was still asleep in the bed next to her. She must have been exhausted last night, Bella realized, for her to have slept so far past dawn.

Bella ran her fingers through her tangled hair, looking around the room. She hadn't gotten the chance to take it all in when she'd arrived so late last night. Her fatigue had taken over and Annie and she had all but collapsed in the bed, still in the clothes they'd traveled in, and fallen fast asleep.

Now she saw that the room was quite simple, in a charming way. The inn, if she remembered correctly, was the only inn they would encounter for some time, which was why the coachman had urged them to stop. It was a quaint thing with a kind innkeeper who had taken one look at them and ushered them upstairs before they even discussed payment. The room itself had all the bare necessities—a bed, a desk and table, a hearth, and a chamber pot. The bed was barely big enough to fit the both of them but Bella didn't think it mattered. They would be gone soon enough.

She let out a sigh, rubbing the crust from her eyes. Annie stirred by her side. Then she shot out of the bed so quickly that she swayed a little once she was on her feet.

"Milady, I must have overslept!" she said quickly.

"Worry not, Annie," Bella said. "After I all but dragged you away from the house last night, I would be a cruel mistress if I didn't let you sleep a little longer."

Annie's shoulders relaxed a little but she stayed standing. "How are you feeling, milady?"

"Absolutely horrible," Bella confessed. She held her head, feeling the onset of a megrim. She hoped it would stay away until she'd at least made it to her mother. "And I'm sure I look a sorry sight as well."

Annie did not say anything, which was all the answer Bella needed. She let out a dry laugh devoid of mirth. She looked around the room once more. "I made a mistake, didn't I?" she asked after a while. "I should not have left."

Annie frowned. "Perhaps we have time to return before anyone notices that you're gone."

"Look at the sun in the sky, Annie," Bella said, pointing out the window. "I'm sure someone has noticed my absence. And hopefully, they've noticed my letter as well. I cannot go back, even if I have realised that I've made a mistake. I shall continue onwards to my mother's side."

"Forgive me if this seems a little forward of me, milady," Annie said gingerly. "But I do not see what running away will do."

Bella gave her a rueful smile. "Delay the inevitable?" she suggested. "I know I cannot escape the consequences entirely. Father will follow me and the rumours will not cease just because I am not there to hear them. The truth is that..." Bella trailed off, unwilling to say the words aloud. She'd thought about it before they'd arrived at the inn but she'd been so tired last night that the full panic at her realization had not been felt.

Now it choked her.

"What is the truth, milady?" Annie urged.

Bella swallowed, not meeting Annie's eyes. "Father will force me to marry Lord Granville."

"Milady, he cannot!" Annie gasped. Bella just shook her head.

"He can do whatever he wishes. He will be thinking about the best way to overcome this scandal, to make sure that I still stand a chance at being married. And Lord Granville still has ties to the Earl of Harenwood. The business partnership he seeks might not be soured if I marry him since it would still be within the family, thought very distant."

"But…after what he tried to do to you…"

"I do not know if Father believes or if he cares to believe. He will only think about what is best for himself and the family name."

It hurt her to say those words. She wished her father would have shown some kind of concern for her well-being as Gertrude had. But he'd only been focused on the damage to her reputation and how it would affect him, not her.

"Still, you cannot marry Lord Granville, milady. You cannot."

Bella forced a smile onto her face, faking bravery. "Why do you think I am running away, Annie?"

Complete dismay overtook Annie's face at those words. But she said nothing more about the matter and Bella was glad for it. She stated that she would go downstairs to fetch clean water for them to refresh themselves and then she left Bella to her solitude.

Last night, before Annie had entered the room, Bella had wanted nothing more than to be alone. She wanted to cry and wallow for as long as she could before she was forced to face reality again. Now she had to resist the urge to call Annie back, not trusting her thoughts to remain on what she needed to do rather than what she'd left behind.

She'd told Annie that she'd run because she knew what her father would have her do. And that was the truth. Partially. Bella wasn't' quite ready to explain to Annie the depth of her feelings for Edward, even though she knew that Annie could tell. Perhaps anyone looking on that night would have been able to tell if they looked closely enough. Anyone except Edward himself, of course. The hurt that had shone in his eyes had likely blocked everything else out.

And she couldn't blame him. The position she'd put herself in…truly, she'd known better even as she'd done it. But despite it all, Bella would not allow herself to regret her motivations. Eleanor was one of the most important persons in her life and she could not live with herself if she'd allowed anything to happen to her.

Bella didn't get out of the bed until Annie returned with a bucket of water. She washed her face and refreshed herself before changing into a less-dusty clothing. She left Annie to do the same while she wandered downstairs.

The inn was empty save for the same kind innkeeper who had assisted them last night. He wiped the counter, unaware of her approach. Bella took in the modest surroundings for a moment before she faced him.

"Good morning," she greeted.

He looked up at her in surprise. He was a middle-aged man with a heavy pouch of a stomach and enough gray in his hair for Bella to believe that he had not led an easy life. Even so, his smile quickly touched his lips at the sight of her.

"Good morning," he greeted. "I half-expected your maid and you to sleep the entire day away."

Bella shifted uncomfortably, not certain how she felt about how easily he'd deduced that they were maid and mistress. She knew she hadn't revealed who they were last night.

"Thank you," she said, "for your hospitality. How much do I owe you?"

"We can talk about payment another time. I'm sure you have more than enough for one night's stay." He tossed his cloth over his shoulder. "Now, are you hungry? When was the last time you ate?"

"You needn't worry about us," Bella assured and tried to ignore the way her stomach grumbled. It had been some time, she realized with a start. "We have to leave soon so we have no time to eat. I'd much prefer discussing payment."

The innkeeper gave her a look of pity. "Oh, you poor thing. He did not tell you, did he?"

"What are you talking about?"

"Your coachman has left. It appears he received a better offer early this morning and took off. Without a word, it seems, since you are looking at me as if it is the first you're hearing about it."

"He left?" Bella repeated incredulously. "How could he do that? How else will we get to our destination?"

"Blame the business," the innkeeper said. "It is a fickle thing that answers to nothing but the jingle of coin."

Bella tried not to show her dismay. Did that mean they were stranded here? Sitting ducks while her father took after them? If she lingered here for too long, she was sure to be discovered. What should she do now?

"You look distressed," the innkeeper observed.

Bella didn't bother to point out that he was stating the obvious. "Is there anyone else who may be able to take me?" she asked even as she looked around the empty inn. She had a sinking feeling that Annie and she were the only current occupants.

The innkeeper confirmed her suspicions by shaking his head. "I'm afraid not. And there is no telling when one will be by. They come often enough, but not often at all at times. I wouldn't want to get your hopes up." He paused, observing her for a moment. "Fill your bellies, at least. A warm meal and some hot tea may help you feel a little better."

Bella doubted it but she wouldn't turn down his kindness a second time. Especially now that she hadn't a clue if or when she would be able to leave.

"I'll fetch my companion," Bella told him and turned woodenly back to the stairs. She knew he watched her as she ascended but she didn't focus on that. Her mind whirred as she tried to find a solution to her problem and came up short. The best she could hope for now was that another stagecoach would come by soon.

She prayed she would not be discovered before then.

***

Edward woke with a splitting megrim, a dry tongue, and a throat that burned. He pulled himself upright, his back and neck aching from the uncomfortable position he'd slept in all night. The dried tears on his cheeks cracked as he tried to stretch then gave up halfway through at the pain that assaulted him.

He didn't mind it entirely. Physical pain was good. It was decent distraction.

He pulled himself to a stand, fighting the wave of dizziness that assaulted him. As much as he hated how he felt right now, he didn't regret his night of indulging. With the dead weight that hung in his chest, beating so low and slow that Edward wondered how he was still standing, he wouldn't be surprised if he turned towards brandy tonight as well.

But right now, he had to at least pretend to be fine.

He'd made it a few steps before someone banged on the door. Edward groaned aloud, clutching a nearby end table as he growled, "Go away."

"Edward, open up!" Amelia called from the other end. "We have to speak. It's urgent!"

"I'm not falling for that, Amelia," he said. "Leave me be."

"No! I shall stand here and bang on the door until you open up." The banging began. Edward trudged over to the door, knowing very well that this was a battle he couldn't hope to win.

He pulled it free and leaned heavily against it as he looked at his sister. "What."

Amelia looked horrified at the sight of him. So much so that she didn't say anything at first. When her eyes began to water, Edward rolled his eyes and walked away, leaving the door ajar for her to enter.

He made his way back to the chair he had slept in and tried to keep his eyes from pounding out of his skull.

"Say what you want then leave," he ordered brusquely. "I am in no mood for company."

"I can see that," Amelia murmured. She approached slowly, sinking onto the chaise lounge across from him. "I'm so sorry that this has happened, Edward. So terribly sorry."

He didn't want to hear it from her. There was a blond-haired, green-eyed lady who should be saying those words. Edward closed his eyes and exhaled slowly in the hopes that it would rid the image of her from his mind.

But all he could see were her tear-filled eyes pleading with him to see something he could not. To believe her lies.

This time, the pain that hit his chest had nothing to do with his physical afflictions. He glared at his sister with just a minute amount of guilt. "Enough stalling, Amelia. What do you want?"

His cold tone did not upset Amelia as much as he thought it would. "I overheard something that I think you should know. It's about Lady Isabella—"

"I don't want to hear it."

"Edward, just listen to me, will you? Lady Isabella did not—"

"Enough, Amelia!' he barked. She flinched. "I said I do not want to hear. I have severed my ties with that lady and that is that."

"And you've made a grave mistake by doing so," Amelia insisted. "She did not do what she has been accused of. It was all planned."

Edward frowned at her. Despite what he'd said, he asked, "By whom?"

"Aunt Catherine and Thomas." It looked as if it pained Amelia to say those words. "I overheard them speaking this morning in the parlour. Thomas was telling Aunt Catherine that he had to think on the spot to figure out how to lure Lady Isabella outdoors. And Aunt Catherine was commending him, telling him that he did a splendid job and his method did not matter as much as the result."

Edward sat up straighter at that, feeling dizzy even though he was sitting. If this was true then that meant...

"Lady Isabella was telling the truth," Amelia stated. "She did not do what everyone suspects her of doing. She'd been put in a compromising position by Thomas and was not even given the chance to explain herself."

"I did give her the chance," Edward murmured though he hardly heard himself. "I did but she said nothing."

"You demanded to know what was happening in front of so many onlookers," Amelia told him. "And you had clearly believed the lie already. We all did. But now we don't."

Edward stood. The room spun around him. "This doesn't make any sense," he pushed out. "Why would Aunt Catherine do this?"

"She hates Isabella's mother," Amelia explained softly. "I overheard how she thought it was fitting that Isabella would suffer the way her mother should have all those years ago. And Thomas just laughed saying that he didn't care if she suffered, as long as he married her and used her dowry to pay off his debts."

Rage surged through Edward's body, chasing away the pain. He clung to that anger to absolve himself of the guilt that threatened to consume him, however brief it was.

"Edward?" Amelia sounded so far away, her voice tinged with worry. "What will you do?"

"The thoughts that are running through my head are not things a lady should hear," he growled through gritted teeth. His hands turned into fists at his side in an attempt to contain his anger but all it did was promote it.

"I understand that you're angry," Amelia said in a calming tone. "I am as well. I consider Lady Isabella my friend and even if I did not, it upsets me that anyone could play with someone's life like that. If someone had not stopped them when they did, I shudder to think what would have happened."

It was not lost on Edward that this someone had been Catherine. Had she followed them out there? Had she watched in the shadows as Thomas forced himself on Isabella? The mere thought transformed his fury into something so tangible that it restarted his dying heart.

"I think you should go to Lady Isabella, Edward," Amelia said after a long while. "Before you seek revenge, I think you should seek forgiveness. I could see how heartbroken she was after all you'd said."

Edward remembered it so clearly too. He had almost clung to that glimmer of hope that perhaps things weren't how they appeared. If he had, perhaps this could all have been avoided.

But, as Amelia said, he hadn't given her much of a chance to explain herself. He'd demanded something of her that she could not give in the moment and then had severed their connection with such force that it left them both reeling.

"What if she does not want to see me?" he asked his fear aloud.

Amelia touched him lightly on his arm, making him jump. He hadn't heard her approach. She gave him a warm smile. "She will. If what I think is true, she feels the same for you as you do for her. She will forgive you, Edward, if you give her the chance to."

That was all he needed to hear. He pulled Amelia close, kissing her fiercely on her forehead before he rushed out of the room to win back the love of his life.

Chapter Twenty-Four

Edward all but threw himself off his horse and thanked God he didn't twist his ankle on his landing. He patted the horse and told him to stay as he rushed up the steps. Taking a carriage would have taken too much time. A horse was faster.

He resisted the urge to bang his hand on the door, remembering his manners. He knocked and waited impatiently for someone to answer him. When the butler opened the door, Edward stepped inside.

"Where is Lady Isabella?" he demanded hurriedly. "I must see her. Show me to her now."

Something flashed across the butler's face, gone a second later. "Lady Isabella is currently not available, my lord," the butler informed him.

"Not available?" Edward's heart sank. Did she tell the butler to say that if he came to visit her? Edward looked desperately towards the staircase and contemplated going in search of her himself. "Relay a message for me then. Tell her that...that I…"

What could he say now? He'd raced over here knowing that he had to make things right but he hadn't a clue how to go about it.

The butler looked a little hesitant before saying, "Forgive me, my lord, but I am unable to do so at this time."

"What do you mean by that?"

The butler appeared a tad uncomfortable as he opened his mouth to respond. But someone else spoke instead. "It means just as he has said, my lord."

Edward breathed a sigh of relief at Lady Wentworth's approach. Her cat strolled next to her and the fluffy feline instantly began weaving between Edward's legs, purring loudly. Had the stakes not been so high, Edward would have reached down to pet him.

"I'm afraid I do not understand, my lady," Edward confessed. "Has she refused to see anyone. Or has His Grace forbidden that she can be visited?"

Lady Wentworth's face did not give anything away. As she stared at him, Edward could not determine if she was on his side or against him. "Follow me, Lord Belmont," she said after a moment then turned and walked away.

Both Edward and Mr. Whiskers trailed after her. Edward tried to quell his anxious energy as he entered the drawing room and watched as she calmly took a seat. It appeared as if he had interrupted her breakfast. Edward hadn't even considered the fact that he was coming here at an improper time.

"Please, have a seat, my lord," Lady Wentworth offered.

Edward didn't want to have a seat. He wanted to see Isabella. But because his only path to seeing her sat before him, he did as he was told. He tried not to hide how impatient he was becoming but Lady Wentworth regarded him as if she could see right through him.

"Isabella has run away," she said without warning.

Edward was suddenly grateful for the chair because his feet would have given way underneath him. "What?" he breathed. "What do you mean, she's run away?"

"Just as I have said." She was calm, too calm for the magnitude of her news. "I found a letter in her chambers early this morning. In it, she explained that she was unable to bear the weight of all that has happened and wished to escape it all."

"Did she say where she was going?"

"She did not."

Edward couldn't believe his ears. Certainly this was a mistake. Or perhaps he was dreaming. He couldn't possibly be sitting here talking with her aunt about the fact that the love of his life had run away from home as if they were simply discussing the weather.

When he finally overcame his shock, the questions flew from his lips without stopping. "Have you sent out a search party? Is there anything missing from her chambers? Is there anyone missing from the servants? Have you questioned any of them about what they might know? Have you contacted the constable?"

Lady Wentworth took her time in answering. She sipped her tea daintily then set it down before looking him in the eye. What he saw took him by surprise.

She wasn't just calm. She was worried and simply trying to hold herself together. Her measured words, her practiced movements, her stiff shoulders. All of it hid the fear that shone in her eyes, even if that fear was absent from her voice as she spoke.

"I have sent out a search party but nothing has come of it yet, nor do I expect anything to. The only thing missing from her chambers are a few articles of clothing. Her maid is missing as well which leads me to believe that Isabella asked her to come with her. I have questioned the servants as a group and have asked for anyone who knows something to come forward. It came as no surprise that no one did since I'm fairly certain Isabella made her decision late last night, after everything that transpired. And no, I did not contact the constable. I have not deemed it necessary. Yet."

Edward shot out of his chair, unable to keep still any longer. "What of the duke? What has he done to—"

"His Grace is unaware of the situation, I'm afraid. He left for a business trip early this morning, before Isabella's disappearance was discovered." Lady Wentworth sipped her tea again. Edward wondered if she did it to center herself. "I am grateful that you are here, my lord. You see, I was quickly running out of options."

"I shall find her," Edward stated firmly.

Lady Wentworth chuckled. "I admire your tenacity, my lord. Especially since you haven't a clue where she could have gone."

"Your tone makes me wonder if you do."

Lady Wentworth nodded. "She did not state it in her letter but I know my niece better than she thinks. She will not run off to live by her lonesome. I know she misses her mother and sister dearly, so I am certain that she has left for her sister's countryside manor."

That was all Edward needed to hear. "Thank you, my lady. I shall make sure to bring her back."

"That is all I ask for, my lord. Hopefully before her father catches wind of her actions, though I doubt we will be so fortunate." Lady Wentworth stood. "Before you leave, my lord, there is something I must say to you."

Edward nodded and braced himself for her next words. She had every reason not to like him, he knew. If she knew the truth behind what happened, then his reaction would have undoubtedly soured her impression of him.

So it took him completely by surprise when she said, "I believe you to be an honorable man who cares deeply for my niece, my lord. Your actions, though done out of hurt, displayed your feelings clearly. I am entrusting my niece to you."

"Thank you, my lady," Edward responded, grateful beyond words. "I will not let you or Isabella down again."

"I certainly hope not," she said. Her rueful smile was the last thing he saw before he raced out the door once more.

***

He had been riding for hours but the time seemed to pass so quickly that he barely noticed it. The only reason he did was because the sun was high in the sky by the time he spotted his first landmark.

For a moment, Edward considered riding right past the inn. He'd gotten directions to Bella's sister's manor and he wanted desperately to bridge the gap between them. He didn't want to slow down for a moment.

But then it occurred to him that Bella might have stopped at the inn. She couldn't make the trip in one day. And even if he wanted to do just that, the same went for him. His stallion might be beast but he would collapse underneath him if Edward didn't give him water and time to rest.

He gave it little more thought before he turned off the road and brought his stallion to a slow stop in front of the inn. It was a small thing with no stagecoaches outside. That didn't give him much hope. He desperately prayed that Isabella hadn't made the foolhardy decision to make the trip by horse in her haste like he had.

He patted his horse and told him to stay before making his way into the inn. The innkeeper straightened upon his entrance. "Welcome," he greeted. "What can I do for you? A bed? A warm meal?"

"Just water for my horse and information if you have it," Edward said. "I am looking for a lady. She has blond-hair and green eyes. She's a petite figure and is about this tall." Edward put his hands against his shoulder. "Has she been here?"

The innkeeper tilted his head to the side. "And who might you be, sir?"

The question threw him but Edward saw no reason not to indulge him. "My name is Lord Edward Harrington, Viscount of Belmont. The lady I seek is...my betrothed."

"Why would you be looking for your betrothed here?" he asked Edward. "If a lady thought to run away to keep from marrying you, I see no reason why I should tell you where she is."

Edward stared at the innkeeper for a moment. He wondered if the innkeeper understood that he'd basically given away the fact that he knew of Isabella. "Where is she?" Edward pressed.

"I shan't tell you," the innkeeper stated, crossing his arms.

Edward walked away, heading for the stairs. He didn't need the innkeeper to tell him. This was a small inn. If Isabella was here, he would find her.

"Oi! You cannot go up there!"

The innkeeper scrambled after him but Edward's strides were longer. He made it to the top of the staircase before the innkeeper even began his ascent. There were five rooms he realized.

"Isabella?" Edward shouted, banging on the closest door. "Isabella, are you here?"

"Are you out of your mind?" The innkeeper finally caught up, heaving. "No one is up here!"

"Isabella!" Edward continued. Desperate now, he didn't care about propriety. He was almost certain that she was here. He began throwing the doors open, the pangs of disappointment growing stronger when he found each room empty.

"I told you," the innkeeper panted behind him, "that no one is here. So if you'd please leave my establishment!"

"Forgive me, good sir, but I shall do that when I find her." Edward stepped past the man as he bumbled for a response. He made his way back downstairs, looking around for anywhere she could be. He spotted a door that looked as if it led to the back of the inn. He hadn't a clue why Isabella would be back there but he made for it anyway.

"Sir!" the innkeeper raced after him but was too late to stop him from throwing the door open.

The door led outdoors. Wind hit his face, the sun stinging his eyes as he tried to adjust to the sight before him. The inn, small as it was, sported a garden next to the stables. Edward headed there.

He didn't have to get very far before he spotted her.

Relief seized him so fiercely that he didn't know whether to laugh or cry. He ran instead, charging past the rickety gate that tried to bar him from the gardens. Isabella noticed him when he was almost upon her, her eyes widening with surprise. He didn't give her a chance to say anything before he swept her off her feet, burying his face into the crook of her neck.

"I'm so happy I found you," he breathed against her flushed skin. He finally set her down, looking into those big, beautiful, confused eyes.

"Edward," she breathed. "What are you doing here? How did you find me?"

"I heard that you had left home and came searching for you," he explained. He didn't want to let her go and she clung to his arms as if she did not want to either. "I decided to stop here to rest for a while and inquire about whether you had passed through."

"But...why?" She still looked so confused and a little wary. Edward wanted to kick himself for putting that look on her face.

"I..." He trailed off when he realized that they had an audience. There was another woman standing nearby. Likely the maid Lady Wentworth had spoken about, further evidence by the way she bowed deeply when their eyes met. The innkeeper had caught up as well and was panting heavily behind them.

"I tried to stop him," the innkeeper attempted to explain to Isabella.

"Thank you, Robert, but it's fine," she said gently. She looked back at Edward. "Shall we speak inside?"

He nodded wordlessly and forced himself to step away from her. He hadn't gotten her forgiveness yet, he reminded himself. He couldn't overstep. Not if he wanted to keep her.

Chapter Twenty-Five

Bella didn't dare to let herself hope. She sat across from Edward in the main lobby of the inn under the wary and watchful eye of Robert, who stood in the corner of the room. To her surprise, the innkeeper had developed quite a liking for her, evident in his over-protectiveness.

Annie sat a few tables away pretending as if she was still not close enough to overhear the intimate conversation that was about to ensue, like a proper chaperone.

Edward fiddled with his fingers and then ran them through his hair. He was nervous, Bella realized, which confused her even further. Why should *he* be nervous after what *she'd* done?

"I don't know how best to say this," he began eyes flitting to hers then away. "I apologise for the way I spoke to you, Isabella. And for not believing that there might have been more to story than met the eye."

Bella didn't dare to let her hope grow. She'd been so certain that her relationship with Edward had come to a definite end that she didn't want to feel that all over again. The disappointment, the hurt. "Did Lord Granville tell you what happened?" she asked carefully.

Edward shook his head. He looked horrible, Bella noticed again. He looked as if he hadn't slept at all last night and he hadn't stopped to run a brush through his hair before leaving. Still he was so handsome that it hurt a little to look at him.

"The truth was that Catherine was behind it all along," he confessed, lowering his eyes as if he had reason to be ashamed.

Bella expected the shock, though the force of it was not nearly as earth-shattering as one might think. After all, Lady Catherine and she had never been on the best of terms before. Bella had simply assumed that the older woman had just grown bitter and overbearing over time but perhaps there was simply more to the situation than what met the eye.

She voiced her confusion aloud to Edward but he shook his head sadly. "It involves your mother, though I do not know the specific nature of her hatred towards your mother exactly. I am just as shocked by this revelation as you are. Catherine is many things but I did not think she was capable of sabotaging one's reputation for her own satisfactions. Believe me when I say that once we return to London, I shall demand the truth."

Bella licked her lips, trying to calm her raging heart. Too many things were swirling in her mind at once and she grappled to maintain her composure, to keep from growing overexcited with the possibilities of what he might be suggesting.

"Isabella." The gentle call for her name quieted her thoughts for just a moment as she met his eyes. They were filled with desperation. The sight sliced through her defenses. He reached across the table and laid a hand atop of hers. The simple yet tender touch all but seized her heart in his grasp all over again. "I know I have wronged you. I understand the role I play in what transpired last night. But please, I need you to know that I am terribly sorry for it all and that I will do what I must to atone for my sins."

Despite the seriousness of his words, Bella's lips twitched. "You make it sound as if you have wronged me in many ways, Edward."

"It feels as if I have," he confessed seriously.

Bella longed to entwine her fingers with his, not caring if the innkeeper was still watching them. "You are forgiven, Edward, though I do not think there is any for me to forgive. I do not blame you for the way that you reacted nor do I blame you for ending our engagement. Despite the fact that it was all orchestrated, my reputations had been torn to shreds. I understand if you no longer wish to be associated with me."

Bella lowered her gaze to the wooden table as she spoke. She wished she didn't feel any shame. She had nothing to be ashamed about, after all. But sitting across from Edward like this, so close to baring her heart and soul to him, brought so many waves of emotions she didn't know how to handle. And she certainly didn't want him to see them.

"Isabella, do you think I raced all the way from London on horseback in search of you simply to issue an apology?" Edward asked softly.

Bella looked back at him with a frown. "No. You wish for me to return to London as well, though I have no intention of doing so."

He shook his head. His hand tightened around hers. "Isabella, I'm here to take back all I said before. I was too blinded by my hurt to see the truth but eventually I would have realised that I cannot live without you. You have changed my life so irrevocably that the thought of you leaving, tears me to pieces."

"Edward..."

She didn't want to get her hopes up. Even as her heart hammered madly against her ribcage, as her insides somersaulted, as her cheeks grew hot and the breath in her lungs grew shallow, Bella didn't dare to assume what he was trying to say. Even though it sounded as if he was trying to tell her...

"I love you, Isabella." Shyness had his eyes flicking away for a second, before meeting hers once more. "And I cannot imagine a life without you in it. You have brought meaning to my existence. Where before I was a shell of a man going from day to day pretending I was fine, now I have a true purpose. It is to love you. And if you deem it fit, to be loved by you."

Bella parted her lips to respond but nothing came forth. It seemed he had stolen her ability to speak as well.

Edward shook his head and she could tell he was forcing the smile onto his face. "There is no need to tell me if you do. There is only one answer I seek from you. Isabella...will you marry me?"

Bella wished she could tell him her true feelings. But her throat closed instead, burning with the tears that shimmered in her eyes. All she could do was nod.

A grin split Edward's face in two. That sight was enough to make everything that happened almost worth it. He shot to his feet with renewed vigour.

"Then we shall continue on with the journey," he said. "Lady Wentworth is expecting me to bring you back to London before your father finds out that you've left but I know you well enough to know that it will not be so easy to change your mind. I shall wait here with you for a passing stagecoach and then we'll—"

"Edward." Bella stood. Without thinking, she reached back for his hand, entwining their fingers as she had been longing to. He looked down at it in surprise and she waited for him to meet her eyes again before she said, "I love you too."

No one mattered in the next few moments. Bella didn't care about the innkeeper, about Annie, about maintaining propriety. All that mattered was that she would marry the man she loved. That the man she'd given her heart to smiled at her as if she were the sun and he was wilting flower desperate for its warmth.

That the man who had set out to win her back was now dipping his head towards hers.

Their lips met with soft urgency. It was her first kiss and it was gentle and as perfect as she'd imagined it would be. It ended far too quickly for her liking and when he pulled away, Edward must have noticed the longing in her eyes. He chuckled softly, resting his forehead against her.

"You've just made me the happiest man on Earth," he whispered.

"Good," she whispered back. "Because you've made me the happiest woman."

Chapter Twenty-Six

The innkeeper—Robert—did not like Edward in the slightest. At first, Edward had assumed it was because he did not trust Edward's intentions towards Isabella—though why he felt so strongly about a lady he'd just met was beyond Edward's understanding—but even after he'd proven that he was not a threat to her, the innkeeper was no kinder.

Isabella found it endlessly entertaining. She didn't bother to hide her giggles as Robert sent scathing looks Edward's way but sweet and gentle ones to Isabella. While they waited for a stagecoach, he served them a hot bowl of meat soup. Isabella and her maid, Annie, received hearty portions filled with meat while Edward's bowl was nearly all broth.

It didn't bother him quite that much, however. Nothing could upset him right now. The day had begun with a dark cloud of despair hanging low over his head, threatening to erupt. And now it felt as if the sun had come out and he was bathing in its warm rays.

Isabella was the sun. She was everything to him. And he would be damned if he'd let anything come between them ever again.

Which meant a confrontation must be had soon. When they returned to London, he intended to get the full truth from his aunt's lips. As for Thomas…well, he didn't really care to understand his motivations. Thomas only acted in his own self-interest.

Edward couldn't deny to himself that his aunt's betrayal cut deep. Now that he had mended things with Isabella, the weight of what she'd done settled heavily on him. He knew how prickly she could be but he'd never once thought her to be an evil woman. What she'd done to Isabella though was nothing short of that. How could he have let someone like that go near Isabella in the first place?

He told himself not to think about it anymore, not until he was in London again. By midday a stagecoach came by and they were able to commission it to take them the rest of the way, with his horse trailing dutifully behind. As Isabella, Annie and he climbed into the coach—under Robert's watchful eye—Edward felt a tremor of nervousness of what was to come.

Isabella must have sensed it because she took his hand once more. Ever since her confession, she stayed close to him, seizing every opportunity to touch him. This was no different. Not that he minded at all.

"What are you thinking?" she asked him.

"About what's to come. Meeting your mother and sister. Facing your father. Facing mine."

"We have each other so there is no need to worry." She said it so simply, as if it were but a fact that he only had to accept.

Edward grinned. He supposed that was that.

The trip extended for a few hours, long enough for the women's exhaustion to overtake them. They both fell asleep, Isabella's head rested against his shoulder. She snored, he noticed with a smile. Soft and gentle.

He didn't dare to move, in the fear that he might wake her, until the carriage pulled up to a manor. He gently stirred them both awake. Isabella opened her eyes groggily while her maid instantly sat upright as if she had been awake all along, her cheeks coloring. Edward paid the coachman and then accepted Isabella's things.

The driveway was long and washed in grass, the manor sitting to the back of the estate. Despite that, their arrival had not gone unnoticed. Footmen approached and, upon seeing Isabella, they immediately began escorting them to the manor's entrance.

Word must have gotten around quickly, Edward realized. The moment they walked into the foyer, a lady heavily with child screamed from the top of the staircase, "Isabella, what are you doing here?"

"Matilda, be careful!" Isabella rushed forward but Edward was quicker. In long strides, he ascended the steps and offered a hand before she could make her descent. She looked at him in surprise, hand sliding into his.

"Thank you, sir," she breathed. She cupped the bottom of her large stomach and began waddling down the stairs with

Edward's assistance. Isabella met them at the base with a broad smile.

The moment Edward let go of the lady's hand, the two sisters embraced each other with such fierceness that Edward grew a little concerned for the unborn child for a second.

"Matilda, I'm so happy to see you," Isabella breathed, her relief evident in her voice. When she pulled away, her eyes shimmered with happy tears.

"As am I to see you, Bella!" Matilda exclaimed. A frown furrowed her brow. "But what are you doing here? Don't you have a wedding to plan? The last I heard, last night was to be your engagement ball, wasn't it?" Before Isabella could respond, Matilda slapped her on the arm. "And why have I been receiving news about you through Mother? Did it not cross your mind that I would wish to receive letters from you as well? It is bad enough that Mother and I could not be there but now—"

She broke off, looked at Edward as if she hadn't remembered that he was standing there. Any other lady might have been a little embarrassed by her tirade in front of company but she only turned to face him, both hands supporting her belly.

"Forgive me," she said in a calmer tone. "I do not believe we have met."

"Matilda, this is my..." Isabella blushed and Edward grinned. "This is Lord Edward Harrington, son of the Earl of Harenwood and Viscount of Belmont. Edward, this is my sister, the Marchioness of Avandale."

"It is a pleasure to meet you, my lady," Edward greeted politely, bowing. "Isabella has told me much about you."

"And yet I have heard almost nothing about you, my lord," Matilda observed, sliding a scathing look to her sister. "But I'm sure that will all be remedied in short order. It's a long journey from London. Why don't we relax in the drawing room. You two are just in time for tea."

"Where is Graham?" Isabella asked. She slid her arm through her sister's as they walked, slightly ahead of Edward. "And Mother?"

"Graham is on a business trip and will not return until tomorrow morning. And Mother is somewhere within the manor. She will hear that you are here soon enough."

"Graham is Matilda's husband," Isabella explained to Edward. "The Marquess of Avandale."

"It is a small world, my lady," Edward said to Matilda. "Your husband and I have met quite a few times. He visits the club I frequent in London."

"Is that so? A small world indeed." Matilda sounded intrigued but left it at that. "So tell me, Isabella, everything that has happened in London. I want every sordid detail. You cannot begin to imagine how terribly dull it is having to remain indoors while the Season goes on without me."

"You will be giving birth at any moment, won't you?" Isabella asked, touching her sister's belly. "I cannot understand why you would want to attend any of the Season's events at all."

"This child invigorates me, rather than tires me," Matilda explained. Upon making it to the drawing room, she ambled over to a high-back armchair and struggled to take a seat. "I have so much energy and nothing to put it towards."

"Well, I shall tell you all that has transpired once Mother arrives," Isabella said with a smile. "Until then, tell me how you have fared."

Matilda sighed but indulged her sister. Edward remained standing, observing them. They were so much alike that it was a bit uncanny. They had the same unconscious movements—shifting from side to side as they spoke, fiddling with their fingers. They even looked so similar that Edward would have been willing to believe that they were twins.

In the middle of Matilda telling Isabella about the way their husband tended to her every wish while present, another lady walked into the room.

No, not twins, Edward thought. *Triplets.*

Isabella's mother squealed upon seeing Isabella. Isabella barely had the chance to stand before she was almost knocked off her feet in a fierce hug. Edward couldn't help but smile. Their similarities showed far more vividly in the way they spoke to each other than in their appearances, he noted.

The older woman stopped short when she noticed Edward standing by the window. Her smile fell, her face growing pale. She looked at Isabella in slight horror. "Bella, what happened?" she asked gently.

Isabella's smile slipped from her face. Was it a mother's intuition, Edward wondered, that made her realise that something was amiss so quickly?

"Mother, allow me to introduce you to my betrothed, Lord Edward Harrington of Belmont. Edward, this is my mother, Lady Rosalind, the Duchess of Redshire."

Edward approached and swept into a low bow. "It is a pleasure meeting you, Your Grace."

"Honestly, my lord, I wish that I could say the same," Rosalind said. Edward nearly laughed. Now he knew where Isabella had gotten her bold nature from.

"Mother!" Isabella gasped.

"Now, Bella, I am no fool. As happy as I am to have met your future husband before you two are wed, I get the sense that you are not here to introduce him to us. Look at the state of you two! And you arrived suddenly without sending word, without your father, without your aunt. I'm surprised you even brought your maid with you, though I am grateful for it." Rosalind reached for Isabella's hand and steered her towards a sofa to sit. "Tell me what has happened, my dear."

Isabella thinned her lips, glancing at Edward. He gave her a nod of encouragement. She took a breath...and then launched into a detail rendition of everything that had happened the previous night.

Matilda and Rosalind, to their credit and Edward's slight surprise, did not interject. They listened with focused faces, nodding at some parts of the story as if they were not the least bit surprised. When Isabella was finished they exchanged glances.

"What is it?" Isabella asked, noticing the exchange as well. "Why are you two looking at each other?"

Rosalind didn't answer right away. She shifted closer and enveloped her daughter in a tight embrace. "I'm so sorry this happened to you, my dear. Though I am surprised that you received such unkind treatment from Lady Catherine. Why didn't you tell me sooner?"

"I didn't want to worry you," Isabella confessed. "I know how close Matilda is to giving birth and I did not want my issues to impact either one of you."

"The day you told her is the same day Mother would have been in London," Matilda agreed. "I understand why you did not say anything, Bella, but you needn't worry so much about me. I am not as fragile as you may think."

Rosalind sighed. "Lady Catherine has a very off-putting personality, I agree. We had debuted at the same time, if I recall correctly, and would often find ourselves in the same place. She did not have many friends so I made sure to speak to her often so that she would not feel lonely. I would not say that we were friends, but on good terms. So why would she hate me to the point that she would be taking it out on my daughter?"

She curled her hand into a fist, exhaling sharply. "I have half a mind to go to London and set her straight myself."

"Don't' forget that we have company, Mother," Matilda drawled. She was looking at Edward with a knowing smile. "I take it you know the truth as well, since you are here and not in London nursing the wounds of a broken ego?"

Edward's lips quirked. He had to admire the way Matilda spoke like she did not care about the consequences of her words. "I was the one who learned of it first," he explained. "Once I realised the error I made, I raced after Isabella to beg for her forgiveness. And to ask her to marry me."

"How sweet," Matilda drawled. "So you two did not come together by design?"

"No," Isabella spoke up, though she hung her head. "I ran away from home."

"Ran awa—" Matilda didn't get through the rest of her exclamation. Her face stilled, with only her eyes blinking rapidly. Slowly she put a hand on her stomach. "Mother?"

"Yes, my dear?" Rosalind was by her side in half a second. "What is it? What's the matter?"

"Perhaps Isabella was right about the impact her arrival would cause," she said calmly. She looked up at her mother. "I believe I am going into labour."

Chapter Twenty-Seven

Everything was moving far too quickly. Bella couldn't keep up.

So she sat as still as a stone as anxiety curled throughout her body. Funny how she once thought she'd never felt nervousness before when that emotion seemed to consume her wholly now.

Thankfully, Edward was here. She couldn't remember how many times she had that thought over the hours that went by. As the sun dipped behind the horizon, and her energy sapped to where she could do nothing but sit there, Edward was on his feet. He'd launched into action the moment Matilda made her announcement and did not stop until he had no choice but to leave it in the hands of the professionals. Even so, he made sure Isabella was well. Knowing her worry, seeing it stark on her face and trembling through her limbs, he brought her chamomile tea, a blanket, and offered soothing words to her and her mother.

Everything will be all right. Children are born every day, aren't they?

And many lives were lost during childbirth. Bella didn't want to point out that fact. She only prayed that her sister would be fine.

She didn't know when she fell asleep but was suddenly wakened by her mother's joyful cheer. She mistook it for panic at first and was halfway out of her armchair before she realized what was happening.

"Is that..."

Edward appeared by her side. Goodness, she couldn't remember how not to lean on his strength. "A healthy baby boy," he whispered to her. It was still quite late at night, she realized. Perhaps early morning.

Bella rose, drifting over to where her mother stood with a bundle of joy in her hands. The midwives stood by beaming happily but Bella had to ask to make sure. "Matilda...?"

"She's asleep, my lady," one of the midwives said. "She has exhausted herself but she did wonderfully."

"He's already suckled as well," the other said. "It put him right to sleep."

Bella crept closer. Indeed, the baby was asleep, so at peace that she felt the dregs of her anxiousness fade. A smile stretched across her face as she reached out to take him from her mother's arms. He was so small, so perfect.

"What is his name?" she asked to anyone who would answer.

"She has not named him yet," Rosalind answered. "She wanted to wait until her husband returned."

"I see." She felt Edward come to her side. Bella looked up at him, not realizing that her eyes blurred with tears until they spilled over her cheeks. "Isn't he precious?"

Edward didn't answer out loud, only giving her a small nod and an odd look. She was used to him staring but there was something about the way he studied her holding the child that made her wish that they were alone. So that she could draw closer to him and inquire about his thoughts. So that she could rest her head against his chest and fall asleep.

"We should put him down to rest, Your Grace," one of the midwives spoke up. She stepped forward to retrieve the infant from Bella's arms. Bella felt a pang of longing as soon as she did.

"Yes, and it is late," her mother agreed. "We should retire. Bella, let me walk you to your room. Lord Belmont, the butler will escort you to yours."

Rosalind took Isabella's hand and steered her out of the room before she could say anything. They were already ascending the staircase by the time Edward emerged behind them.

Bella didn't attempt to look back at him, even though she was tempted. Her longing for his company grew the further she was from him. An amazing situation she'd found herself in, she mused. So enamored by a gentleman that the mere thought of parting ways tore at her chest.

But she reveled in her mother's company. She'd missed her dearly while she'd been in London. To be back with her family, to have been fortunate enough to arrive right before Matilda went into labor, made this insane trip completely worth it. So much so that she could almost forget the trouble she would be when her father came looking for her.

"Honestly, Isabella, what were you thinking?"

Her mother only ever called her by her full name when she was excited or disappointed. Bella couldn't tell which she was right now.

"I was thinking," she sighed, resting her head on her mother's shoulder as they walked, "that I did not know what to do anymore. I was frightened, Mother. I was afraid of what would happen the morning after the engagement ball."

"Your father's actions will be even worse when he finds out that you've run away from home," her mother stated.

Bella nodded and sighed again. "I have been trying my best not to think about it."

"Well, you must. Since you will be returning to London in the morning."

"Mother, I cannot!" Bella gasped, pulling away to look at her with wide eyes. "I only just arrived! And…and Matilda has just given birth! She will need help."

"She will receive all the help she needs from me and her husband," Rosalind stated in a firm voice. "I did not raise you to run away from your problems, Isabella."

Disappointment. Definitely disappointment.

"I am only taking a small hiatus from my chaotic life," Bella grumbled. "I should at least wait until the rumours die down."

"The moment you return to London, they will start back up again. It is a vicious cycle, sadly." Rosalind took Bella's hand, patting it gently. "Do not worry so much, my dear. I'm sure when you return, no one will dare say anything about what happened anymore. It will be old news."

"How can you be so certain?"

"Because you will be returning with your husband in tow."

"My husband? But I'm…" Bella trailed off. Rosalind smiled and they continued along.

"It will not be eloping," Rosalind continued. "Others will only assume that you've mended your relationship and have decided to get married out of the public eye. But, truthfully, Bella there is no reason to be concerned about the opinions of others. You have a gentleman who looks at you as if you are the most precious person in his life and your father would be a fool to be angry with you when your marriage was the only thing he wanted in the first place."

They arrived in front of the bedchamber Isabella often used when visiting her sister. Rosalind held both her hands now, kissing her gently on the forehead.

"My point is, Bella, you need not worry at all. Everything will work out."

A part of Bella didn't believe it. Even though she'd made it to her destination, even though she was happy to be with her sister and mother again, Bella couldn't shed the underlying anxiousness that had been following her the moment she slipped out of her home in the dead of night.

Her mother's words easily shed that dead weight that had been clinging to her. Bella relaxed into her arms, letting her tears slip down her face even as a smile touched her lips. "Thank you, Mother."

"You're welcome, my dear. Now, get some rest. I have a feeling you'll have a busy day tomorrow."

Chapter Twenty-Eight

The last thing Edward wanted to do right now was return to London. Being in the countryside with the lady he loved brought him a sense of peace he hadn't felt in years. He wanted to savor the moment. He wanted to learn everything he could about Isabella and the stories of her past.

Rosalind indulged his curiosity, much to Isabella's chagrin. The moment he came down for breakfast, Rosalind answered every one of his questions and told him story after story about Isabella's childhood. He learned about the girl who would get lost in the forest and cry all the way home when found, only to get lost again the next day. He grew to adore the maturing lady who had decided that spending too much time outdoors was unbecoming of her and tried her hand at watercolors and the pianoforte instead, as a lady should. He laughed when he learned of how Isabella realized that she was not artistically inclined and that her true loves—literature and history—turned her into the bookworm he knew today.

He was so engrossed in the tales of the past that he wasn't prepared when Isabella cut into the conversation to ask, "Why don't we get married before we leave for London, Edward?"

She would never fail to surprise him.

At first, he'd only stared at her. That adorable blush of hers coated her cheeks and her mother smiled as she lifted her tea to her lips.

"Pardon me?"

Bella nervously averted her eyes for a moment and then met his again. "I thought it would be a good idea," she explained. "It may make our return a little easier to digest and keep the ton from gossiping too much."

"Isabella..." Edward was at a loss for words.

Bella reached for her cup of green tea a little clumsier than usual. "If you would like to wait, then I have no issue with that. If you still wish to be marri—"

"I want nothing more than to become your husband," he said quickly, surprising her. Her cheeks grew redder. Her Grace laughed quietly behind her hand but Edward only had eyes for his betrothed. "We can marry right now if you wish. The sooner I can call you my wife, the happier I will be."

A shadow of a smile passed over Isabella's lips. "If only it were that easy."

"It can be." Now it was his turn to blush but he didn't look away from her as he continued. "I acquired a special license. On the night of our engagement ball, I had intended to confess my love for you and show you the depth of my love by showing you the license, even if you wished to wait before we were married."

"You...what?"

"How sweet," Rosalind spoke up. "I'm sure that is what my daughter wished to say."

"And so much more," Isabella breathed. "So we can get married tomorrow then?"

"Today, even," he said a little too eagerly. Her face cracked into a wide smile as if she could no longer hold it back. "If you wish it."

"I do! Let's get married today."

Edward wanted to pull her into his arms and kiss her until the world fell away. Perhaps, had her mother not been present, he would have. He just barely managed to restrain the urge as he returned her grin. "Let us begin then, shall we?"

***

Bella could hardly believe how quickly everything was happening. The parson was contacted and informed about the decision while Bella was whisked upstairs to get pretty. Anna and her mother fussed over her ceaselessly until every bit of her had been primped and polished. Within an hour, she was being ushered downstairs to the waiting carriage that would take her to the church.

Edward waited for her at the carriage. He helped her inside with a broad smile, murmuring about how lovely she looked. Bella could hardly contain her heartbeat. She wished to respond in kind but her mother climbed into the carriage behind her and the moment was lost.

But she didn't take her eyes off him. And he didn't take his eyes off her. So many promises passed in the short span of time it took for them to arrive at the church. Promises for the love they would give each other, for the life they would create.

No words needed to be exchanged as they made their way into the church. The parson and his assistant stood by waiting for them. It was small, simple, yet perfect. The only thing Bella regretted was that Matilda was still on bed rest and could not be here.

But she promised herself that this would only be the formality. A ceremony with everyone Edward and she loved would be necessary for the future.

For now, Bella only wanted to truly become his.

She took his hands, hardly listening as the parson began the reading from the Book of Common Prayer. It was modified since there were no guests to address but it hardly mattered to Isabella. She listened with half an ear as she took in Edward—the curve of his brow, the crook of his lips, the shine of his eyes. She loved him. In truth, she did love him.

Bella wanted to say as much when it came her turn to say her vows. She repeated what was said to her by the parson and then Edward did the same. Soon enough, the parson announced that Edward may kiss his bride.

And kiss his bride he did. He pulled Isabella close, smiling as he lowered his lips to hers. Bella was grateful that he held her because her knees grew weak, her heart pounding so rapidly against her chest that she was certain he could feel it. When he pulled away, she was a little unsteady still.

It was perfect. So perfect, Bella thought as she clung to Edward's arm and they followed the parson to sign the marriage papers.

Nothing could make her unhappy anymore. Not even the bitter lady in London who had set out to ruin her life.

Chapter Twenty-Nine

"I wish you didn't have to leave so soon."

Edward turned away from the window, looking at the scene before him. Isabella leaned over her sister's bed and pressed a kiss on her cheek. "I will return before you know it," she said. "There are some things I need to take care of and I cannot run from it any longer."

Matilda laughed. She looked much better two days after giving birth. Her husband sat by her side—and had been there since he'd returned yesterday morning and learned that his wife had gone into labor without him present. Even though Matilda clearly looked fine, the marquess appeared anxious, a worried frown touching his brow when Matilda attempted to sit up.

"I can hardly believe that my sister has gotten so mature," Matilda laughed.

Isabella rolled her eyes, bringing a smirk to Edward's lips. "I am a not a child any more, Matilda."

"Yes, yes, so you would like for me to believe," Matilda teased. She looked over at Edward. "Why are you so far? Come here."

Edward did so, a bit sheepishly. He'd wanted to stay close to Isabella while she said her goodbyes but hadn't wanted to intrude on a tender moment, which was why he stayed by the window.

"Take care of my sister," Matilda said in a firm tone. "She likes to act stronger than she really feels."

"Matilda!"

Edward smiled. "My only purpose in life is to make sure she is happy and cared for."

Matilda smiled. "Good. Now, go on. And don't forget to visit as soon as you can."

"I will." Edward didn't miss the shine of tears in Isabella's eyes when she responded. "By the way, Matilda. Have you decided to name your son yet?"

Matilda looked at Graham and they shared a smile before she said, "Charles," she said. "His name is Charles."

Isabella nodded and wiped her tears, finally turning away. Edward gathered his crying wife in his arms the moment the door closed.

***

The trip to London, with Isabella's maid in tow, felt much quicker than the trip away. They stopped at the same inn they had last time, much to Edward's chagrin. But Isabella was eager to tell Robert all about what had happened. It came as no surprise that Robert was not very happy with Edward after learning the fact.

They arrived in London within two days and the carriage took them straight to the Redcliffe residence. A footman ran out to meet them while another raced off, no doubt to inform the duke of his daughter's return. Edward had expected this much. And even though Isabella's shoulders were tense and her eyes filled with resolve, she did as well.

What he did not expect was to walk into the foyer and come face to face with his family as well.

Humphrey, Catherine and Amelia were standing in the foyer along with the duke and Lady Wentworth. Lady Wentworth and Amelia were the only ones who looked relieved at the sight of them and the latter even rushed forward, throwing her arms around Edward.

"I was so worried about you!" she cried. "When I heard from Lady Wentworth that you had left London, I didn't know what to think!"

Edward returned the embrace. He pulled away and frowned over Amelia's head at Lady Wentworth as she approached. "You did not tell her?"

"I'm sure you can understand why I would not," Lady Wentworth said calmly. She went straight to Isabella's side and, to his wife's surprise, pulled her into a hug. "Isabella, you scared me. I didn't know what to think."

"I'm sorry for worrying you, Aunt Gertrude," Isabella said softly. "It was immature of me."

"Quite so," Lady Wentworth agreed. She pulled away and whispered, "I hope you are ready to explain yourself."

"I am," Isabella stated. Then she looked up at Edward.

He contemplated taking her hand at that moment and dragging her out the door so that they could put this off a little while longer. Seeing his father reminded him of what he had left behind and he wanted to remain in the bubble of happiness he'd been in being away.

Instead, he nodded and together they approached their fathers.

Fury roiled off the both of them with such force that Edward nearly faltered for a second. Then his aunt stepped forward and he remembered the role she played in everything that had happened.

He was not prepared, however, for her to step forward and slap Isabella across the face.

Lady Wentworth surged forward, putting herself between Isabella and Catherine. Amelia gasped loudly somewhere behind them. Humphrey threw his hands up as if he could not be bothered with the high emotions in the room.

Edward hardly noticed any of it. His fury consumed him so wholly that it took every bit of his strength to keep from lashing out.

"Are you out of your mind?" he pushed through gritted teeth.

"Are *you* out of *your* mind?" Catherine shot back. "How could you let this woman lure you away after what she has done?"

"Do not talk about my wife that way!" Edward bellowed. "You are the reason all of that happened! You are the mastermind who put her in that position in the first place! You did nothing but throw rocks and hide your hands!"

Catherine's eyes went wide, looking from Edward to Isabella. He didn't dare to look back at his wife. If he saw a red mark on her cheek there was no telling what he would do.

"Wife?" Catherine echoed. Then she looked at Humphrey. "Do you hear this madness? Surely you would not allow him to marry a lady with such a scandal attached to her name?"

"From what I am hearing, it sounds as if you are the cause of that scandal, Lady Catherine," the duke spoke up, his voice nothing but a growl. "Explain yourself."

"There is nothing to explain. She tells him lies and he is foolish enough to listen to her."

"Lady Isabella isn't the one who told him, Aunt Catherine," Amelia said. "I overheard your conversation with Thomas about what happened. You were saying how happy you were that everything went according to plan and that you hated Lady Isabella's mother so much that you wanted nothing more than to sabotage her daughter's life. And then Thomas said he didn't care what your motivations were as long as he got to marry Lady Isabella and use her dowry to pay off his debts."

The color drained from Catherine's face.

"Do you dare to deny it, my lady?" Isabella asked coldly. Edward finally chanced looking at her. Indeed, her cheek as red, but her eyes were filled with such cold determination that he knew he didn't have to worry about her.

"L-lies," Catherine stammered. "Nothing but—"

"Enough!" Edward roared. "I shall listen to this no more. You are a disgrace, Catherine. I cannot believe that I could not see you for who you were sooner."

"How dare you!"

"The truth! Tell us the truth or else you shall regret it."

Catherine balked. She looked like an animal trapped in a corner and realizing that there was no way out. The indignation on her face was replaced with fear, then annoyance, then resignation, then anger.

"So what if I orchestrated it?" she hissed. "It matters not to the ton now. She will always be disgraced in the eyes of those who matters. And it serves her and her conniving mother right too."

"What does my mother have to do with any of this?" Isabella demanded to know, her voice cracking in her anger.

"Everything!" Catherine screamed. "She has everything to do with this! She has haunted me my entire life! Everything that was meant to be mine was stolen by her! The attention! The family! The title! Even the man I was meant to marry!"

"Oh, I do not believe this," Victor muttered, seemingly annoyed with all of this.

He was the only one who didn't appear surprised by Catherine's unintentional revelation. The rage seeped from her face as she realized what she'd just said. "It doesn't matter now. I do not love him any longer."

She was only making it worse for herself, Edward realized. But he couldn't find it in himself to care.

"I do not see how I can trust you again after all of this," he said in a cold tone. "The only reason I'm not exiling you from my life is because, at the end of it all, we are family. And had it not been for me, you would have been pauperised a long time ago. You should take care to remember that. Now apologise."

Catherine pulled her shoulders back, her eyes flaring with defiance.

Edward was about to speak again when he felt a hand on his arm. He looked down to see Isabella at his side.

"I do not need her apology, Edward," she said softly, not taking her eyes off Catherine for a second. "Now that I know why she did it, I pity her. I do not forgive her, and I shan't forget, but I am willing to let go of it all now."

"I don't need your pity," Catherine spat. She looked at everyone with wild eyes. "I do not need any of your pity."

She gathered her skirt in her hands and marched by, charging right past the front door. They all watched her go in tense silence before Humphrey broke it with a sigh.

"Now that that is over with, I need a drink. Your Grace, do you care to join me?"

"You read my mind, my lord," Victor agreed. He didn't move straightaway, giving Isabella a piercing look. Edward felt a glimmer of pride when she met it unflinchingly. "We have much to talk about Isabella."

"I'm sure we do," she agreed and watched him walk off.

Edward faced his wife. In the corner of his eye, he noticed Lady Wentworth guiding confused Amelia away and he was grateful for it. He palmed Isabella's hurt cheek. "How bad is it?"

"Not bad," she said with a smile. "She is not very strong."

"She should not have dared to put her hands on you in the first place," Edward seethed.

"That is true. But I shan't stay upset about it. Now that the truth has been revealed, I'm just happy we can put this all behind us."

"You do not care about what your father wishes to speak with you about?"

"I do not." She sighed and stepped into his arms. "I only wish the manor was empty so that we can truly be alone."

Edward cradled her head against his chest, breathing her in. "You forget, my love, that we are man and wife. And I do not live here. Neither do you, if you do not wish it."

Isabella pulled away just enough to give him a broad grin. "I have something else in mind first."

"Oh? What's that?"

"The British Museum," she said. "You owe me."

Epilogue

One Month Later

"Beautiful! Absolutely beautiful!" Matilda broke off with a sob.

"Oh, heavens, there she goes again," Rosalind laughed. She held out the handkerchief she had no doubt brought to Bella's chambers for this occasion. "Wipe your tears, Matilda. You know how splotchy your cheeks get when you cry."

"A wedding is an occasion meant for tears, Mother," Matilda said even as she reached for the handkerchief. "And this handkerchief will be soaked through by noon."

"Let us hope not," Bella said from her spot in front of the vanity table. She idly watched Annie's deft fingers twine her hair into elegant curls as she listened to the commotion behind her. "You always come down with a cold whenever you cry too much."

"Do not worry about me," Matilda said dismissively. "This is your day. Your beautiful, beautiful day."

Bella laughed. "I'm sure you can recall that Edward and I have already been married, Matilda. I am only having his ceremony for your sake."

"Either way, I am happy for you," Matilda sighed. She sank onto the bed and noisily blew her nose. Bella laughed. Matilda had always been the first to forgo her ladylike upbringing whenever she was relaxed. Or overwhelmed.

It wasn't entirely the truth, Isabella thought. Yes, she had considered having an actual wedding ceremony once Matilda was no longer on bed rest. It had bothered her that her sister hadn't been there to see her get married. But it wouldn't be fair to pretend as if this was entirely for Matilda's benefit. Bella wanted this just as much too. She didn't realize how much until she was planning the wedding.

Lady Catherine had overshadowed everything before that Bella didn't realize there would have been such joy in creating this perfect day. They were in the countryside, at Matilda's residence. During the preparations, Bella had wanted only two things for certain—that it be held at the quaint chapel on the estate and that the entire chapel be covered in as many lilies as they could find.

"Matilda is being a little overdramatic, I agree," Rosalind said with a laugh. "But I am happy that you've decided to do a proper wedding, my dear. And you look beautiful. Edward will not know what to do with himself when he sees you."

"It wouldn't be the first time," Matilda said before Bella could respond. "He looks at you as if you were an oasis and he is a man dying of thirst."

"How poetic," Bella murmured as her cheeks colored. Even after a month she still blushed when she thought of him. She wondered when that would stop happening.

"Yes, I am on par with Shakespeare himself," Matilda laughed. "Now, are you ready? The ceremony will be beginning soon."

Annie had just made the finishing touches by the time Matilda finished speaking. Bella rose and Rosalind approached her with a bouquet of lilies. "You look beautiful, my dear," she told her with a kiss on her cheek.

"Thank you, Mother." Bella accepted the bouquet as a smile flitted across her lips. "Isn't it odd that I am a little anxious?"

"I think it would be odder if you weren't," her mother assured.

Arm in arm, they left the room and made their way outdoors. The chapel was already teeming with guests by the time they arrived. Bella knew that Edward was waiting for her inside, that her arrival would mark the commencement of the ceremony. Her sister and mother left her by the door to claim their seats.

Bella drew in a deep breath, letting it out her nose. Everyone she loved was in attendance to witness this event and she was grateful for it. More than that, she was just happy to be doing this the right way, to celebrate her love for Edward publicly.

She just hoped she didn't make a fool of herself by tripping down the aisle.

It was a foolish fear that became quite real the moment she stepped inside and her eyes landed on him. He was all she could see as she stepped forward. Not the parson, not the guests but the love of her life.

It felt as if she was all he could see as well.

Bella floated to the pulpit and did not hesitate to put her hand in his. She felt a faint sensation of deja vu when the parson began and she instantly ignored him. She knew the procedure by now and would simply wait until it was her turn to say her vows. For now she was content to get lost in Edward's eyes.

At last the time came. Her voice rang loud and true throughout the chapel as she recited her vows. When his turn came, Bella felt every word he spoke deep within her heart.

And, before long, it was time to kiss the bride.

Their first kiss as man and wife had been chaste and tender, capable of igniting a flame deep within. This kiss set her entire body on fire.

Edward slipped his arm around her waist and dipped her as he met her lips. Cheers rang through the chapel.

He pulled away slightly and gave her a smirk. "Did that make your heart flutter?" he teased.

"More than you know," she answered honestly, reaching up to kiss him again.

It was better than she could have imagined it. The people, the setting, him. Bella could hardly believe that there was a time when she had been dreading this very moment. Now, she wished she could do it all over again.

***

The wedding breakfast was well underway by the time Edward felt the urge to leave. He looked across the dining room at Isabella, willing her to notice him. She was too engrossed in a conversation with Lady Eleanor and Amelia to realize his plight.

He sighed. Luke came to his side and nudged him in the shoulder. "Why do you look so down on a day like today?" his friend asked.

"I am anxious to leave this place and spend some time with my wife," Edward answered honestly. "I'm sure no one would miss us."

"Do you want me to fetch her then?"

"No, leave her be. She's enjoying herself." That was the only reason Edward was still standing where he was and not crossing the room to get to her.

"I have been meaning to ask you something, Edward," Luke spoke again.

The seriousness of his tone was unlike him. It was enough to make Edward frown. "What is the matter?"

"It isn't anything serious," Luke said with a shrug. "I was only wondering if you would mind if I courted Lady Amelia, that is all."

"Lady Amelia?" Edward parroted. "My sister, Amelia?"

"Yes, do you know of any other?"

Edward only blinked at him. Surely that wasn't what he'd heard.

Luke let out a breath. "I have fancied her for some time now. She's grown up right under my nose and I hadn't noticed. She will debut next year, won't she? I'm sure you won't mind. I would have asked Lord Harrington but I doubt he will see much issue of our courtship since he's always had a soft spot for me. It's you I wonder about since you have always been protective of your sister and you see me as a rake—"

"That is because you are one. And you are rambling."

Luke laughed uncomfortably. "Am I? Is that a bad thing? Does that mean you are against the idea?"

Edward thought about it for a moment then shook his head. "Under normal circumstances I would have said no, but you clearly seem very anxious about this. It makes me wonder if you truly do have feelings for my sister."

"I do. I would not lie to you about that."

"Then by all means, you may. If she wishes it. And I hope you do not mind me saying that I pray she does not."

Luke laughed, his serious façade gone. "I don't think we have to worry about that. Now, if you will excuse me."

He walked off, heading in Amelia's direction. Edward watched as he said something to her and she giggled. He realized a second later that Isabella was no longer standing next to her.

"My lord?"

His heart skipped a beat at her voice. He turned, a smile stretching across his face to match hers. "Yes, my lady?"

"You look a little tired of this event. Shall we leave?"

"You read my mind, my love."

Together, they slipped out of the dining room. Edward draped an arm around her waist as they made their way to the foyer.

"So tell me, Isabella," he said. "Was your wedding everything you dreamed of?"

"It was and even more. My only wish was for there to be lilies. And a man I truly cared for."

"I'm happy to have made your dreams come true." And because he could not help himself, he kissed her on top of her head. He didn't have to look to know that she was smiling.

"Do you think she would have been proud?" Isabella asked. "Your mother, I mean. Do you think she would have liked me?"

"She would have loved you."

"My brother would have loved you too. I know it."

"Good. I'd hate to face him in the afterlife with a bad impression already." He stopped as they made it to the front door. "You are everything to me, Isabella. And I will spend the rest of my life making sure you do not doubt it for a second."

"As will I." She melted into his arms. "I love you, Edward."

"I love you too, Isabella. You are my heart."

This time, the world did disappear, if only for a moment. In that moment, nothing else mattered. Not the pains of past nor the uncertainty of the future. All he cared about was now. This moment where it was only the two of them and their love that would stand the test of time.

Extended Epilogue

Five Years Later

Children were a handful. Isabella had always known that in the back of her head. She'd been told it many times over by her own mother who never missed a moment to say how much of a troublemaker Isabella had been in her childhood. But living it was an entirely different ordeal to hearing about it.

She could do nothing but stand and watch as her rambunctious four year old toddler attempted to climb the mantle yet again. He would be unsuccessful, she knew, which was why she didn't bother to to move. She'd taken him away from the hearth four times already and he'd only gotten up and waddled back over there. She had to admire his determination.

"Theresa," Bella called wearily. "Please make sure that Henry does not hurt himself. And I think Kate needs to be changed."

"Yes, my lady." Theresa, the governess, surged to her feet. Isabella watched as the homely women scooped Henry into her arms and try to shush the toddler as he wailed in protest. Kate, the ever gentle two year old toddled who idolized her older brother, quietly accepted Theresa's hand.

"The dinner party is still underway," Bella said as the governess approached. "But I will come by later to tuck them in for bed."

Theresa smiled. "Yes, my lady. I shall make sure that they are ready."

Bella nodded. She looked at her rebellious son and her kind daughter and said, "Do not give Mrs. Jones any trouble, all right?"

"I want to climb!" Henry wailed.

"I want to climb too!" Kate echoed.

Bella sighed. "Would you like for me to come with you?" she asked Theresa.

The governess quickly shook her head. "No! No need, my lady. I can handle them on my own."

"Very well." Bella turned to the door, then went back to kiss both her children on their foreheads. "Be good, all right?" she said to them.

They stayed quiet until she was out the door. Then the wailing began.

Bella sighed. She was tempted to go back in. She'd left her dinner party in the first place because her motherly instinct had told her that something was amiss. And she'd found her children racing through the hallways, giving their governess a difficult time.

Bella had stayed with them for nearly an hour, reading to them, playing with them, and then watching them play by themselves. Now that she was gone, they were mourning her absence in the way only children could. By crying.

It took much of her strength to walk away and head back to the dining room. The moment she did, she felt her trepidation melt.

The room was alive. Her father and father-in-law sat by the sideboard with full decanters, glasses heavy with brandy, and cards in their hands. She didn't have to guess to know if they were already inebriated.

Her sister-in-law, Amelia, and her husband, Luke, were engaged in a hearty discussion with Matilda and Graham. Which was really Amelia and Matilda going at it while the men stood by and shook their heads at their ladies.

Gertrude was playing the pianoforte and Mr. Whiskers—the darned cat had snuck in again—ran her feet with a surprising bout of energy. Rosalind stood by, swaying along.

And then there was Edward...and Catherine.

Bella didn't know why she'd allowed her to come. She hadn't forgiven her for what she'd done. Years later she was yet to receive an apology. Catherine had simply acted as if she'd done nothing wrong, even while she was ostracized by nearly everyone in the family.

So when Edward said that she'd reached out to him recenty, Bella didn't care to wonder why. It didn't cross her mind for a second that Catherine was ready to mend her wrongs.

Yet as she looked at them speak, she wondered if she might have been wrong about that.

As she approached, Edward noticed her and said, "Here she is. Say it yourself."

"Say what?" Bella asked.

Catherine actually looked…uncomfortable. Bella couldn't believe her eyes. "It is long overdue," Catherine said, a little meekly. "I can hardly look you in the eye as I say it."

"Are you going to apologise?" Bella couldn't help but ask, incredulous.

Catherine's eyes shot to the floor. "Yes. These past few years have showed me how wrong I was and…nothing I say can change the past. But I would also like to say that I am…grateful for your graciousness in allowing me to attend this evening in the first place."

It looked as if every word she spoke was akin to swallowing nails, Bella observed, humored by the fact.

"I cannot deny that it may take a while to accept your apology, Catherine," Bella confessed. "But…you are willing and that is what matters now."

"That is all I need." Catherine lifted hopeful eyes to the room. "I only hope that the others see it the same way."

They had all ignored her all evening so Bella doubted it would be that easy. "I'm sure they will soon enough," she said instead. She noticed a fluffy tail drawing closer and smiled. "At least one of them are willing at least."

Mr. Whiskers bumped his head into Catherine's leg. The older woman recoiled. "Shoo!" she hissed. "Go away!"

Mr. Whisker's meowed and the devilish genius showed her more affection rather than his usual crankiness. Catherine raced away and Mr. Whiskers took after her.

Bella laughed, stepping closer to Edward. "An unusual sight, isn't it? Catherine and Mr. Whiskers being nice."

"The times are changing, my love," Edward agreed with a grin.

Bella took his hand. "Follow me into the gardens," she suggested.

He didn't hesitate to do just that. Everyone was so caught up in what they were doing that they didn't notice when she left the room a second time, with Edward in tow. Quietly, they made their way to the gardens, awashed with moon and starlight.

They headed down a cobbled path hand in hand, silently admiring the stars above.

"Is there something on your mind, my love?" Edward asked at last.

"Yes," she confessed. "I am considering the best ways to tell it to you."

"Just say it straight," he suggested. "That is what usually works best for me."

"Very well." Bella could no longer fight her grin. She had been keeping this secret for days, waiting for the right time. "Do you remember the list of names you had when we were naming Kate?"

Edward nodded, bemused. "Yes, I had them for both boy and girl—" He broke off, eyes growing wide at her knowing grin. "Don't tell me...?"

"I am with child, my love. We have been blessed once more."

She hardly finished her sentence before he picked her up with a shout of excitement, twirling her around. Bella laughed as he set her back down.

"What shall we name her, Edward?" she asked.

"Her?" he echoed breathlessly. "How do you know it will be a her?"

"Mother's intuition?"

Both their laughter was cut short by his lips on hers. It was a while before they came up for air.

"Have I told you I love you?" Edward whispered to her.

"Almost every day. And it isn't nearly enough."

"I love you, Isabella."

"And I love you, Edward."

They kissed again, with the stars watching. A perfect moment that she never wanted to end.

The End